"I thought you liked women with spirit."

Eden had been too angered by his arrogance to keep silent.

"Ah," he replied softly, "spirit, yes, but that's not quite the same thing as we've been talking about, is it? To me, spirit in a woman means love and loyalty. She can be as good as a man, but she doesn't have to kill herself or him trying to prove it."

Eden frowned. The combination of his closeness and the turn of their conversation had unsettled her. "It seems you don't like career women," she said hesitantly. Wouldn't you marry one?"

Vern smiled and shook his head. "Not the ambitious kind. But I'd give the right woman my name, my protection and my love."

"That's sounds ideal," said Eden sadly, "but too many men fall short of the ideal."

MARGARET PARGETER
is also the author of these

Harlequin Presents

and these

Harlequin Romances

These books may be available at your local bookseller.

For a free catalog listing all titles currently available,
send your name and address to:

HARLEQUIN READER SERVICE
1440 South Priest Drive, Tempe, AZ 85281
Canadian address: Stratford, Ontario N5A 6W2

MARGARET PARGETER

caribbean gold

Harlequin Books

TORONTO • NEW YORK • LONDON
AMSTERDAM • PARIS • SYDNEY • HAMBURG
STOCKHOLM • ATHENS • TOKYO • MILAN

Harlequin Presents first edition October 1983
ISBN 0-373-10638-6

Original hardcover edition published in 1983
by Mills & Boon Limited

CHAPTER ONE

THE calypso band was good, as was the atmosphere in the Country Club, set on one of Jamaica's lush tropical beaches. Because Eden hadn't expected to enjoy herself she was surprised to find she was having fun. She hadn't danced for almost two years, not since Vern went away, but she refused to spoil this evening by thinking of him. He had ruined so many moments of happiness for her simply by imposing himself on her memory. It must be time she learnt to forget him and began living again!

The lively dance finished, and she laughed when the boy she was with asked if she was thirsty. Nodding ruefully, she said she wouldn't mind some lemonade. 'Something long and cool, anyway.'

Leon grinned, reluctantly releasing Eden from his strong young arms. 'Wait here,' he said quickly, 'I'll see what I can find.'

Without much interest, her smile fading, Eden watched as he hurried away. Leon was twenty, the same age as herself, a nice boy who worked in one of the many hotels dotted over the island. She had only met him an hour ago when Fay Derwent, the friend she was with, had introduced them. Eden wondered why he didn't make her heart beat faster. Then her glance swung and collided dramatically with that of the only man who ever had.

Shock exploded through her immediately, and briefly everything went dark. Praying she had made a mistake, she blinked and looked again, but it was Vern. Her face went white as her eyes became fixed on his and she saw nothing in them but mockery. Another man was talking to him, obliging him to look away, but not before she had recognised the old familiar contempt etched on his hard, handsome features.

Vern Lomax—his name began beating in her head until she felt ill. He was supposed to be in the States. Why had he come back? It must be to check on the plantation, but she hadn't thought to see him again. Recalling his brutality on the last occasion they had met, Eden shivered.

From a great distance she heard Fay enquiring anxiously if something was wrong. 'You've gone quite pale, Eden.'

Fay's insistence broke the trance Eden was in, the anxiety in Fay's voice forcing her to pull herself together. 'I'm fine, Fay, really I am.'

'You're sure?' Fay, considerably older and feeling responsible for having persuaded Eden to come here this evening, still frowned doubtfully. 'I hope I can believe you. You look as if you've just received a shock of some kind.'

'It's nothing,' Eden replied unsteadily.

Fay didn't notice Eden's tightly clenched hands, but she did absorb something of her hidden tension. 'Robert's asked me to dance,' she said uncertainly. 'Will you be all right until I get back?'

'Of course!' Eden hastened to assure her, while finding it painful even to breathe.

'Where's that boy Leon got to?' Fay glanced round impatiently, then suddenly exclaimed. 'Is that what it is? Has he upset you?'

'No, no!' recognising Fay's determination, Eden panicked. With Fay there had to be a reason for everything, and if she sensed a mystery she seldom stopped until she got to the bottom of it. If she didn't escape heaven knows what Fay might manage to get out of her, and Eden felt she would rather die than confess how, after twenty-three months and eighteen days, the sight of Vern Lomax still had the power to disturb her. 'Leon went to get me something to drink, but I expect there's a queue at the bar. Actually, I think I'll go home ...'

At once Fay pounced. 'So there is something?'

'It's just my head's aching.' It was beginning to, but Eden was ashamed of using it as an excuse. If Vern hadn't been there she might have ignored it, but his presence, which she was sure was the cause of it, made it imperative that she left as soon as possible. She was certain he would have no desire to approach her, but it was a risk she wasn't prepared to take. 'You won't mind, Fay?'

'No, not if you're really feeling ill.' Fay stared at her closely while the faithful Robert hovered patiently. 'I'd rather you stayed, though, you might feel better in a few minutes if you sat somewhere quiet. You're only twenty, Eden. You should be enjoying yourself and unwilling to go home before dawn.'

'I was enjoying myself.' Eden willed herself not to look at Vern again.

'Were you?' Fay frowned dubiously. 'I thought you were too, and if you weren't it's not the fault of at least half a dozen young men!'

'Robert,' Eden forced a teasing smile, 'won't you take her away? She's fussing me!'

'Me, too,' Robert grinned conspiringly.

'If you do decide to leave, and I wish you wouldn't,' Fay implored, taking no notice of Robert other than to throw him a disapproving glance, 'you must let Job drive you home. It's far too far to walk, but I wouldn't put it past you to try.'

'I promise. Oh, and if you see Leon would you please tell him I'm sorry?'

Eden waited a moment until at last Robert managed to prize Fay away, wondering what she had ever done to deserve such a friend. Not that Fay was a friend exactly, but she did buy things from her to sell in her gallery. It was through this that she had made Fay's acquaintance. Eden's painted shells and trinkets sold well. Tourists liked them and for Eden the money was very useful. Without the few dollars she earned, she and her father might easily have starved.

Swiftly Eden turned to leave the overcrowded room, but before she had got more than a few yards, to her dismay she heard a deep voice asking, 'May I have this dance, please?'

Eden almost jumped as a hard hand caught her arm, bringing her to an abrupt halt. The fingers which controlled her were steely and she would have known the voice anywhere. It wasn't necessary to look up to recognise Vern Lomax, but she could no more have prevented her glance from winging upwards than she could have stopped the world going round.

'Hello, Eden,' he looked at her with a smile that didn't quite reach his eyes. 'It's been a long time.'

'Yes.' Her nod was jerky, clearly agitated, although she tried desperately to remain indifferent. At this stage it was no good wishing she hadn't been so confident he would stay away from her. Perhaps his thirst for revenge was still not satisfied.

'Let's dance,' he said curtly.

'I—I'm sorry, I can't,' she stammered, unable to even bear the thought of being in his arms again, 'I'm on my way home.'

'What is it, a fire?' he taunted, his eyes cool and suddenly full of the same contempt she had noticed earlier. It had been in his eyes the last time they had met. Perhaps that was how she recognised it so clearly.

'A headache,' she retorted stiffly. 'Now, if you'll excuse me——?'

'I think not,' he muttered, his glance going insolently over her. 'If you won't dance then I'll see you home.'

'Oh, no, thank you,' Eden managed to reply evenly, 'it's already arranged.'

'Come off it, Eden,' he drawled dryly. 'You know Fay won't mind who you go home with.'

Between clenched teeth, Eden said, 'How do I make you believe I prefer my own company?'

'You didn't always.'

Did he have to mention that? 'I'd rather not talk about the past. What happened then doesn't interest me any more,' she retorted.

'Indeed?'

With his cold, condemning tones ringing in her ears, Eden rushed outside, the hurt of the arm she had wrenched from his grasp nothing compared to the pain in her heart. It was very obvious that Vern hadn't forgiven her for the terrible things he believed her guilty of.

In the parking area at the rear of the Club, she was dismayed to find he had followed her. Why couldn't he leave her alone? Didn't he realise how much she had already suffered?

As she approached Fay's car he strode past her to speak to Job. 'Tell your mistress I'm seeing Miss Rossiter home.'

'Yes, sir, Mr Lomax.'

Job, smiling lazily from the comfort of the back seat, where he waited for Fay, dozed off again happily. Eden felt like shaking him for being so eager to shelve his duties, but if she did he might only appeal to Vern, and she knew who would win. Keeping a rigid control over limbs inclined to tremble, she allowed Vern to guide her in the direction of his car. In the space of seconds they were both inside it and he was driving away.

The moon hung low over Jamaica that night. It looked yellow and threatening rather than romantic. Eden shivered, her muscles aching from being unable to relax. Glancing at Vern, she found the iron cast of his profile less than reassuring.

'I can't imagine why you're doing this,' she cried. 'Haven't you done enough already?'

'If you mean because of what you did—no. I didn't even get started.'

'Vern!' She tried to swallow her pride and appeal to him, for she didn't think she could stand much more. The two years since she had seen him might never have been and it terrified her to realise she was still as vulnerable. 'You told me what you thought of me after the—the accident. What more can you want?'

'It's not what I want, it's what you can do,' Vern Lomax retorted explicitly. 'I brought Jessie back with me. She still walks with a bad limp and could do with a little company.'

Eden went cold. 'I suppose you'll always blame me.'

'Who else would I blame?' His voice was as hard as the set of his jaw. 'I've forgotten nothing, Eden, so don't try and get out of it. Jessie has suffered a lot and if you're asked to help I'd advise you not to complain. Remember it wasn't your legs which were smashed when you crashed the car, and be grateful.'

And that wasn't the worst that had happened! Vern didn't mention it, but what had happened before the car crash had done even more damage, if in a different way. On both occasions it had been his sister and her boyfriend who had been responsible, but Jessie could still have told him nothing.

'I'm sorry,' Eden whispered, her face white. 'We all hoped that the operations Jessie had in the States would make her completely well again.'

'They couldn't work miracles.'

Eden tried not to hear the underlying pain in his voice. 'Now I know you're back, I'll certainly call and see her.'

'Very generous of you,' he replied sarcastically, obviously unaware of the effort it cost Eden to make such an offer.

'If you let me know when it's convenient . . .?'

'We can discuss that some other time,' he broke in harshly. 'Tonight I didn't intend approaching you about anything. I'm afraid I gave way to impulse which tomorrow I'll probably regret, but I had a sudden urge to discover what it is about you that men can't resist.'

The road wasn't good, but the car swiftly devoured its dusty miles. Eden felt startled as she gazed blindly at the roadside palms, their leaping shadows. Vern's question in itself might not be insulting, but the manner in which he delivered it certainly was. 'I don't think men find me that attractive,' she replied coldly.

He immediately contradicted this, and not very kindly. 'At the dance back there, they were around you like flies.'

'You exaggerate!' Eden was suddenly surprisingly angry. 'I don't know when you arrived, and while I admit I did dance with a few boys I know, not one of them made a pass at me. Not,' she added fiercely, 'that it would be any of your business if they had!'

'It's incredible,' he jeered softly, for all the world as if she had never spoken, 'how you do it. Your dress might be clean, but that's all there's to recommended it, you're not even very good-looking.'

'Thank you.' Eden tried to sound indifferent so as not to betray her real feelings. She was well aware of her own shortcomings, but once Vern had told her frequently she was beautiful. Once he had admired her slender figure and soft brown hair, her thin face and wide, bluey-grey eyes. Now he obviously despised her.

'Don't they know what a little tramp you are?' she heard him ask tauntingly. 'Or perhaps they know only too well?'

Eden flinched, feeling the hate in him, a desire to hurt. He was hurting her, his barbed words striking her almost physically, yet what could she say in her own defence? Circumstances were black against her and

there was still no way she could absolve herself without
implicating Jessie, and Jessie must surely have suffered
enough. Besides, Eden thought bitterly, even if she did, at
this late hour tell Vern the truth, would his lack of faith in
her make it worthwhile? Wouldn't it be better to leave
things as they were? It wasn't likely he would stay long,
but while he was here surely the dull numbness she had
built up over the past two years would return and protect
her until he went away again? What purpose would be
served if they went on tearing each other to pieces?

'Please, Vern,' she protested unevenly, 'I can't see any
point in this conversation. Whatever I choose to do, I'm
sure you can't be interested.'

'Not interested,' he agreed curtly, 'curious, perhaps.
After all, you're little more than a child.'

'Hardly,' she flung back, anger stirring again as she
found every word he spoke wounding, 'It must be
because you're nearly forty that I seem young to you.'

'Thirty-five!' he shot her a chilling glance but she
sensed he was also annoyed with himself for caring if
she thought him ninety. 'You still look seventeen.'

'I was eighteen when you left.' When he had said she
was old enough to be married.

'So you were,' he murmured, as if he'd had no idea.
'It's been over two years, hasn't it, and you still appear
remarkably unscathed by your adventures.'

'Why don't you say lovers?' she whispered, goaded.

Vern threw back his head with a bark of harsh
laughter. 'And I always believed you were such a
delicate little thing! It was scarcely possible to touch
you, let alone mentioning anything as evocative as a
lover, without making you blush. All over,' he added
with a rough kind of frankness that made the blood run
cold in Eden's veins.

'It wasn't like that,' she said bleakly, as they drew up
outside her father's ramshackle old house. The ten miles
from the resort might never have been.

'Time distorts even the best of memories.' He turned his head, allowing his glance to trail over her dispassionately. 'You still have an incredibly beautiful body. If I have one regret it's that I didn't take what was offered before other men did. A dead passion can't be revived, but regret can take a lot of getting rid of.'

Eden must have stared into Vern's green eyes for several seconds before realising what she was doing. His opinion of her was shattering, she had never thought it was as bad as that! An anguished sound escaped her as she groped to open the car door. It didn't budge, and she looked at him again, helplessly.

'It's electrically operated.'

How could he sit there, talking so coolly? She had to get away from him before she was ill. Her heart was beating too quickly and something about Vern's narrow regard made her feel frightened. He hadn't even glanced at the door but answered her silent query automatically, as though only one small part of his mind was concentrated on it.

'Please,' her blue-grey eyes were mutely appealing under feathery winged brows, 'let me out.'

'Of course.' Smoothly he pressed a button, but was round to her side of the car almost before she had moved, waiting for her as she straightened to stand beside him.

'Thank you for bringing me home, Vern,' she said, determined he shouldn't find her lacking in manners. He had implied that she had nothing to recommend her, so she must convince him she could still be polite. Briefly she paused, gazing up at him as he loomed above her, his tall, broad body blotting out everything else.

'What is it?' he mocked as she hesitated. 'You aren't expecting me to kiss you goodnight?'

'No!' She fell back as if he had struck her, her thin, finely modelled face white.

'Just as well,' his eyes glinted as he studied her in the moonlight. 'I vowed never to touch you again.'

'I wouldn't want to touch you!' she retorted unevenly.

'Wouldn't you?' His lips stretched mockingly over strong white teeth. 'On second thoughts, it might be a good idea.'

Before Eden could move he bent his head, his mouth crushing hers in what could only be described as a cruel kiss. When he released her she was shaking.

'Don't tell me you're upset?' he quipped, as sudden tears glistened on her hot cheeks. 'Apart from carrying out a small experiment, I was merely giving you what I'm sure you would have received from one of your ardent admirers, if I hadn't turned up.'

A small experiment? Whatever did he mean? Pressing the back of her hand over bruised lips, Eden hated him, hating even more the faint response still lingering deep inside her.

'I was coming home with Job, remember!'

'I suppose any man might do.'

Her hand shot out at that, as his contempt flayed her, making audible contact with his hard face. It was an impulsive gesture, springing from the bitter rage in her heart. Her hand was small but roughened with work and must have hurt from the force she put behind it, but Vern didn't even flinch. His eyes merely mocked her, a glitter in the darkness as she turned and ran from him.

No lights were on in the house. Her father was in bed and all was quiet, the only sound that of Vern driving away, his tyres ripping up the dirt track before he hit the main road.

Damn him! A great sob heaved in Eden's throat, twisting her mouth, contorting the face she rested briefly against the wooden door frame. Desperately she drew breath into her lungs, trying to relieve the terrible tightness in her chest. Was fate never going to be kind to her? Why had Vern come back? The plantation had run well enough without him. He had replaced Diego Dexter with another manager, who seemed to know what he was doing. Since Vern and his sister had gone to the States Eden hadn't been to the house, but her father usually knew what was going on.

Perhaps Vern was just paying a flying visit, although if he had Jessie with him that didn't seem likely. She wondered if he had brought anyone else with him. Vern Lomax had never been short of friends and Jessie had always liked having people around her. Not many had actually stayed on the plantation, though, since their parents had died.

Joe Rossiter shouted from his bedroom, 'That you, Eden? You're early. I heard a car.'

Eden walked down the narrow passage to his door. 'Sorry, Dad, I didn't mean to wake you up.'

'Wasn't sleeping.' Neither of them attempted to put on a light, but Eden heard the springs of his bed creak as he heaved himself higher on his pillows. 'Who brought you home?'

'Vern Lomax.' She might as well tell him, for he would surely find out. Trying to keep her voice steady, she asked, 'Had you heard he was back?'

'Heard something,' Joe grunted. 'Not surprised, of course. He owns a sizeable chunk of land, can't neglect it for ever.'

'George Willis is a good enough manager.'

'Yeah,' through the darkness, Eden could almost see Joe shrug, 'Willis is all right in his way, but there's nothing like the hand of the master. Vern can see with both eyes shut things Willis doesn't see with both his open.'

Eden was too used to Joe's caustic remarks to take any notice. Cautiously she said, 'Vern might not stay long.'

'No, he might not. I wonder if Jessie is with him.'

'He said she was.' Eden swallowed unhappily. 'He— he told me she still walks with a limp.'

Again Joe grunted. 'A wild little piece, that, even if he was always too blind to see it.'

Eden bit her lip. Perhaps it was better than being able to see too much, as her father often did, that was when he took the trouble. 'Jessie can be very nice.'

'When she's getting her own way—just like her mother.'

'Her mother?' Eden had never heard Joe speak so frankly of the Lomaxs before.

'She's was over-fond of having her own way too, and of spending her old man's money. He couldn't deny her anything and she didn't give a care for him.'

'Joe!' Eden spluttered—he didn't like her calling him Dad, 'you shouldn't speak ill of the dead!'

'I'm no hypocrite, Eden. I was as sorry as anyone when they were both killed on their way to Venezuela, but they left Vern a fine legacy of debts. If he chooses to spend what little he has on his undeserving sister, he's a fool, but that's up to him. At least it must prove he's not like his parents.'

'Should I be grateful?' Eden muttered bitterly.

Joe moved irritably. 'What's that, girl? I wish you'd learn to speak up.'

'It was nothing, Joe,' she sighed. 'I didn't know about Vern's parents. To me they seemed just an ordinary couple. Perhaps that's why he's never married.'

'He could have brought a wife back with him. You never know what he's been up to in the States.'

Eden went cold. There had been a girl in the States. According to Jessie, Vern and this girl had almost been engaged. This was one of the reasons why Eden had done nothing to correct the terrible opinion he had had of her before he had gone away.

'If he's here to stay,' Joe added, 'we'll soon find out.'

'Yes, Dad.' Although, suddenly, Eden didn't believe he was married, she pretended to have lost interest. 'I'm tired,' she yawned. 'If you don't mind, I think I'll go to bed. See you in the morning.'

As Joe muttered goodnight, she left him, but in her own room she paused. She knew if she went to bed yet she would only lie tossing and turning, thinking of Vern.

Suddenly her movements distracted, she flung off the dress she was wearing. She didn't care when it tore, though it was the only one she possessed and, because she didn't earn much, she might never be able to save enough to buy another. It was clean, but the pink cotton was faded and shabby. Vern hadn't needed to tell her so. She remembered the first time he had seen it, when he had taken her out on her eighteenth birthday. He hadn't appeared to notice its shabbiness then.

Swiftly she donned a pair of shorts and a shirt and let herself silently out of the house. Running along the beach, she flung herself down on the sands, burying her face in her hands. She wouldn't go in the sea, though her body yearned for its refreshing coolness. It was in the sea that she had had her first real encounter with Vern Lomax, when, thinking she was drowning, he had literally dragged her out of it. Little had she known then that it was to be the beginning of a wonderful friendship, but one which was to last only a few weeks.

'Let go of me, you great brute!' she had choked, struggling against the strength of a man who, to Eden's salt-blurred eyes, seemed twice as large as life.

He took no notice, however, whoever he was, appearing to believe her spluttering protests were the half-conscious ramblings of a delirious mind. His arms tightening about her, he kicked out with his long legs, bringing her ruthlessly ashore. As he turned her face downwards, obviously about to pummel the water and, she suspected, the life out of her, she managed to twist nimbly away from him.

'I told you I was all right, you beast!' she exclaimed, tossing back the wet hair he had grasped so painfully. Her long hair out of the way allowed her to see the face of her would-be rescuer, and she gave a start as she suddenly realised who it was. She hadn't seen much of him for years, but it was the man whose plantation joined their own bit of land running down to the sea.

'Mr Lomax!' her hand flew in confusion to cover startled lips. 'Oh, I'm sorry! I'm afraid I didn't recognise you.'

His eyes held a glint of ironic amusement as he remained where he was, crouched on the sands. 'Does it matter who I am? I shouldn't have thought it would make any difference.'

'Naturally it does,' Eden said stiffly.

'Otherwise, if you hadn't known me, I'd have received a further lashing from your wild little tongue?'

Eden didn't think this was fair. Her brief sense of remorse passing, she retorted resentfully, 'You can't really blame me for being annoyed. Wouldn't you be, if you were enjoying yourself, just floating harmlessly around, and suddenly felt your hair being torn out by the roots?'

'There was a fire at sea, a few hours ago,' he informed her curtly. 'A boat went down, and two people are still missing; I thought you were one of them.'

'I see.' Regretfully Eden lifted her face to the trade winds which were rapidly drying her wet limbs. Wrecks weren't exactly unknown on a coast where thousands sailed each year, but she always hated to hear of a boat going down. 'Do you think there's any hope?'

'Very little, I'm afraid.'

For a few moments they were silent, united in brief compassion until, with a resigned shrug, Vern Lomax said, 'Would you mind looking the other way while I find my clothes? I got rid of them in such a hurry I'm not sure where they are.'

Eden flushed, not having realised he was naked. Quickly she turned to do as she was told, but not before her eyes had jerked involuntarily to his bare body. Most of it was lost in shadows and, relieved but feeling a fool, she hoped he hadn't noticed her apprehensive glance as she stumbled from him along the beach.

Her cheeks went hotter still as she knew she ought to have guessed he had nothing on. Hadn't she felt him against her in the water as he'd drawn her briefly into his arms? For a short time they had been very close, and while he must have believed her unconscious, she certainly hadn't been. Being angry with him had made her forget; now she knew it was something she might always remember!

She had wandered quite a way when Vern caught her up. 'I said to look the other way, not run a mile!'

She caught his teasing smile as she glanced at him. This time she had to glance up, not down, and was startled to notice how tall he was. 'I don't remember you being so tall,' she exclaimed, she thought rather foolishly.

'I don't remember you very much either,' he grinned, then suddenly sobered as his eyes ran over her slender young body. 'You appear to know me, but you haven't told me your name. Would I be right in thinking you're Joe Rossiter's daughter?'

'Yes.' She knew she must sound slightly breathless but something about him was effecting her oddly. 'You know my father?'

'All my life, on and off.'

She smiled at him, suddenly happier. 'You're often in the States?'

'Not really because I want to be,' he replied enigmatically.

Eden almost said, 'Why go, then?' but that might

have been presuming too much, too soon. It was none of her business why he spent so much time in the States and she had no wish to arouse his anger by seeming too curious. Suddenly to have his friendship was infinitely more important than having her curiosity satisfied.

She supposed, like Vern Lomax, she should go and put some clothes on. She didn't feel selfconscious in her brief bikini, which she often wore all day, gathering seashells, but perhaps it might seem more appropriate if she did. Usually, at this time of night she wore her shorts.

They were standing silently, regarding each other carefully. Vern Lomax was studying Eden's face, as if he found the fine bones of it interesting. When she bit her lip, he asked quickly if she was sure she was all right.

'I was until you came.' Eden hadn't meant to say any such thing and to her horror, on top of this, her voice broke, as his concern made her feel sorry for herself again. It had been a disappointing day, but she had no desire to wallow in self-pity.

'Hi!' Vern's hands came out gently to take hold of her. 'You seem upset. I didn't really hurt you out there, did I?'

'No, it's not that.' Despite her efforts to remain calm, tears continued to fall and she rubbed embarrassed knuckles across her wet cheeks.

'Can't you tell me?' She was drawn almost tenderly against a broad shoulder, her damp face allowed to soak his smooth shirt while his hand gently massaged the tension from the back of her neck. He murmured words, as she rested against him, which she didn't quite catch but which she found oddly comforting.

His kindness proved her undoing. On a half sob she confessed, 'I'm just being silly.'

'What about?' he prompted, kissing her tears away softly.

Then it all poured out, as though a gentle kiss, a touch of sympathy, had unlocked a dam of misery. 'It's my birthday,' she told him, 'and no one's realised.'

Vern stiffened, his voice suddenly harder. 'Surely your father . . .?'

Eden didn't let him go on, she pulled away from him, feeling ashamed of herself. 'It's not his fault. He even forgets his own. We usually joke about it.'

'But you didn't find it so amusing just now?'

'No,' she whispered, thinking, with a longing that surprised her, of the arms she had just left, 'but I don't really mind. It was just something that came over me.'

For a moment she thought he was going to argue, then he said quietly, as if he was prepared to go along with this, 'How old are you—today?'

'I'm eighteen,' she replied rather anxiously.

'Eighteen?' A smile lit up his dark eyes. 'Old enough to be married. You aren't, are you?'

'No, of course not.'

'Why of course not?'

Eden gazed at him in the semi-darkness, her spirits rising. That he considered she could be married seemed to indicate that he thought her desirable. Or at least attractive enough to be attractive to someone. Eden checked her churning thoughts with difficulty, refusing to let what he implied, or what she thought he implied, go completely to her head.

'I don't even have a boy-friend,' she revealed unwittingly.

'You mean you've never had one, or you don't have one at the moment?' Vern asked coolly.

She was surprised at his insistence but didn't attempt to lie to him. 'I've never had one,' she confessed.

'I don't suppose you meet many men here.'

'I don't mind,' her soft, sensuously moulded lips tilted happily, 'I'm usually busy. I gather shells and look after the house and my father.'

Vern frowned, but his eyes were gentle again as he watched the varied expressions chasing over her smooth young face. 'You have plenty of time for boy-friends, but not so much for your birthday.' Quickly he consulted his watch. 'You have, in fact, only an hour or two left.'

Puzzled, she followed the movements of his strong, hair-sprinkled wrist. 'It must be almost ten, Mr Lomax.'

'Precisely,' he grinned. 'I can see you're a girl of superior intelligence, after all. And the name's Vern, by the way, in case you've forgotten. I'd like to take you out, but we'll have to hurry if we're going to celebrate— and I'd like to drink your health before midnight.'

Eden's eyes glowed for a moment with innocent pleasure, then as swiftly the glow faded. 'You don't have to ask me out, Mr—er—Vern. I wasn't angling for an invitation.'

'If you don't shut up I'll slap you, young Eden,' he retorted impatiently.

She couldn't remember anyone saying anything like that to her before, and she stared at him open-mouthed.

'Or kiss you,' he threatened, with a wicked drawl, his eyes on her unconsciously parted lips.

Eden drew back, her breath catching apprehensively, then she laughed, knowing she was being silly. 'I'd love to come out with you,' she said, recovering her equilibrium. 'My father's asleep, but I don't think he would mind. I'll leave him a note, just in case he wakes up and wonders where I am.'

'Leave Joe to me.'

His familiar use of her father's name was reassuring. 'I won't have to be late.'

'We won't be,' he promised, guiding her back along the beach and leaving her at her door with instructions to be quick and get changed while he went and sought his car which he had parked on the highway.

CHAPTER TWO

EDEN had just one long dress, and she wouldn't have
had even that if Joe hadn't bought it for her on their
trip, a year ago, to England. The occasion had been the
one evening they had dined with her mother. Joe had
apparently been reluctant to give the impression that he
couldn't afford to have his daughter properly attired.
He always refused to consider her as his ex-wife's
daughter as well as his own, since Iris had left him when
Eden was only three.

Unfortunately he hadn't been prepared to spend
much on what he had blatantly referred to as Eden's
wardrobe, and even after a year the cheap cotton had
faded and appeared, to Eden's eyes, to have lost any
shape it had possessed.

Still, she tried to shrug indifferently, what did it
matter? Here in Jamaica, although it was their home,
she and Joe seldom went out and had no social life.
Since his wife had left him, Joe had grown more and
more into a recluse and his reputation as a well-known
artist hadn't improved. It was true that when he made
the effort he was still capable of producing something
outstanding, but the length of time between such efforts
was growing longer and Eden often felt if it hadn't been
for her sake he might have given up altogether, long
ago. Joe cared for her and so was determined, if
halfheartedly, to keep their home together. He was
always kind to her and because of that she was usually
ready to forgive him anything. And, if she were honest,
apart from being short of money and smart friends, she
found her life, in this lotus-eating land, far from
disagreeable.

23

This evening, for the first time, she felt a flicker of dismay as she gazed at her reflection. Yet the pink dress didn't look too bad, once she had it on and had adjusted the belt a little, and it was unlikely that Vern would ask her out again. The colour suited her, she decided, as she quickly brushed her now dry hair into soft, shining waves and applied a glossy lipstick to her uncertain mouth.

This was all the make-up she had, and Jessie had given it to her. As Eden spent most of every day in the sea and her skin was near-perfect, she had never felt any need to plaster her face with paint and powder, as Jessie did, but she hadn't liked to refuse when Jessie had said it was a present. She realised that, used skilfully, make-up could definitely enhance, but it was an art she had never acquired. It was only because she was going out with Vern that she wished she had had something extra. Some perfume perhaps . . .

She hadn't told Vern yet that she knew his sister. Probably she should have done, but she hadn't had much chance and she didn't think that, to him, it would have made any difference. He wouldn't mind, she suspected, whether she knew his sister or not. Besides, Jessie and she weren't that friendly. Sometimes she wondered why Jessie bothered with her. She was older than Eden and they didn't have that much in common. Jessie was sophisticated and had been around, while Eden, apart from her one trip to England, had never been anywhere at all.

She heard Vern return with his car. He must either have left it quite a way along the road, or been giving her time to get ready. Suspecting the latter, she thought it was nice of him to have been so considerate. He had obviously guessed it would fluster her to have him waiting outside. Of course his concern for the missing tourists proved he was nice. Boat incidents were so common in tropical waters that not many people bothered any more—certainly not to the extent of looking for survivors in the dark.

He knocked on the door, another gesture which gave Eden a warm feeling. He meant to show Joe he wasn't after a clandestine meeting with his daughter. She had told him Joe was asleep, but she admired him for wishing to make sure. She guessed if he didn't speak to Joe tonight, he would certainly be back to do so in the morning.

The door wasn't closed. When she appeared Vern was standing in the opening, his long legs apart, his hands thrust in his trouser pockets in a way that tightened the material over the tautly curved muscles of his thighs. He was a big man, all over, and she wondered why she had never noticed him before.

While his stance might have been careless, the glance he threw over Eden certainly was not. In the dim light of the hall, she heard him draw a sharp breath.

'There's a saying,' he said huskily, as she drew nearer, 'sweet and twenty—but you're only eighteen. Where have you been all my life, little Miss Rossiter?'

This last, even while allied with a slightly teasing smile, brought a return of the strangely tremulous feeling Eden had known on the beach. She looked at him, her eyes like stars, not attempting to hide the quickening sense of happiness his words gave her.

'I've been here all the time,' she laughed, 'but you can't have noticed.'

'People seldom see what's right under their noses,' he agreed wryly, 'but I've always prided myself on being uncommonly observant.' Then, his grin fading, he asked, 'You're sure Joe's in bed?'

'I'm certain.' Her eyebrows quirked ironically. 'Do you suppose he wouldn't be out here if he wasn't? We don't get that many visitors.'

'He never used to be such a heavy sleeper.'

How did Vern know? 'He still isn't,' she sighed. 'He

had a headache and took what looked to be about half a bottle of aspirin, and usually two knocks him out. If you doubt me,' she offered anxiously, 'you can go and see for yourself.'

'No, I'll take your word for it,' said Vern. 'Besides, we'll have to get going, if we intend going anywhere, that is. Come along.'

'Joe trusts me,' she felt compelled to add as Vern propelled her gently outside, closing the door behind them. 'I sometimes go out with friends.'

She wasn't sure if he heard her, because he didn't answer, and she wished she hadn't said anything. Jessie had once invited her on a short sea trip, along with Diego Dexter, Vern's plantation manager, but she hadn't enjoyed herself very much and it had been during the afternoon.

Vern put her in his car, a powerful, low-slung model Eden couldn't remember seeing before. Although she could drive, after a fashion, it was a long time since Joe had possessed a car. Now any car, to Eden, was the height of luxury. Almost reverently she ran a hand over the soft leather upholstery, liking the feel of it.

She glanced quickly at Vern as he negotiated the wide circle of hard, sand-packed gravel which formed a kind of natural drive around the house. She was glad that although he had put on a jacket, he still appeared quite casually dressed. He had made no comment on her appearance and she realised sadly that that might have been kindness on his part, as she must look extremely dowdy. Hadn't Jessie told her frequently that dewy complexions and beautiful hair could be reduced to nothing by unfashionable clothes?

'Where are we going?' she asked, suddenly alarmed that he might be taking her somewhere smart. There were more ways than one of standing out in a crowd and she had no wish to embarrass him.

'Wait and see,' he replied.

'Must I?'

As though he was aware of her nervousness, his laughter, in the darkness, teased her only a little. 'You must, Eden Rossiter. I promise it will be somewhere you'll like.'

'I don't want to go anywhere expensive,' she stammered, hoping he would believe she was thinking of his pocket, rather than of her shabby dress.

Keeping his eyes on the road, watching carefully for straying animals and sometimes people, he asked almost idly, 'What kind of a life do you really lead, young Eden?'

She wished he would stop calling her that, just when she was beginning to feel quite grown up. Glancing at him sideways, her eyes encountered the hard outlines of his face and body and a sensation rushed through her that didn't feel young at all.

'I lead a very quiet life, I suppose,' she admitted unsteadily.

As if conscious of her eyes on him, his own turned to catch hers before she could look away. Something passed between them, nonetheless real for being so brief, as caution forced Vern's attention back to the road.

'Too quiet, I think,' he muttered, half under his breath.

'Why do you say that?' she whispered uncertainly, wishing her heart hadn't begun racing in such an unfamiliar manner. 'I know I was feeling low when you came across me this evening, but I'm usually quite content.'

'Which is a rare quality in a woman,' he noted lightly, after a brief hesitation which might have indicated he was willing to drop his former line of thought for the time being. His mouth quirked. 'A rare quality nowadays anyway,' he amended. 'I think it's all this equality stuff they're being brainwashed with. They have an uneasy feeling that they're missing out on something, that the grass on the other side of the fence is greener. It makes them dissatisfied with what they have while not being sure of what they want.'

He sounded as if he was relating to some kind of personal experience. Eden glanced at him curiously, but merely retorted, 'You talk as though you don't consider I'm one of them.'

Wryly he smiled. 'I don't think you are—yet. You're not old enough.'

She felt strangely hurt by this and replied indignantly, 'If I'm not, I soon will be.'

He sighed, over deeply. 'Now I've said the wrong thing. Just when you've reached the age of maturity. I'll have to beg your forgiveness.'

Eden didn't like the thread of humour in his voice. Not altogether appeased, she said sharply, 'You're very critical of us. I imagine you know a lot of women and speak from experience, at least your experience. What sort of women do you go out with?'

Slanting a glance at her cool profile, he grinned but replied quite soberly, 'I like women who are gentle and feminine, ready to worry over me, rather than my bank balance.'

To Eden this seemed a bit too arrogant. 'I felt sure you would appreciate women with spirit.'

'Ah,' he took a difficult bend expertly as they dropped from the interior hills to the coast on the other side of the island, 'spirit, yes, but that's not quite the same thing as what we've been talking about, is it? To me, spirit in a woman means love and loyalty, a willingness to fight for her family and what she knows is right, but not about every darned thing. She can be as good as a man, but she doesn't have to kill herself, or him, trying to prove it.'

Eden frowned. Their conversation had taken a surprising turn and she wished she had had more experience to argue with him. 'It seems you don't approve of career women,' she said hesitantly. 'Wouldn't you marry one?'

'Not the ambitious kind.' He smiled again, but shook his head. 'You see, child, while women are determined to change, they won't change men as easily. A lot of us still want an old-fashioned wife, who'll concentrate on her house and husband.'

'Don't you think that sounds rather selfish?' Eden asked dubiously.

'Not when you consider what we give in return. Our name and protection, love and a willingness to work, often seven days a week, to keep you in comfort.'

This still seemed a trifle arrogant. Eden's long lashes fell on her cheeks while she considered it. 'You can't believe that's what always happens! It sounds ideal, but a lot of men fall far short.' According to her mother and Jessie, the vast majority of them did!

'Yes, I realise,' Vern agreed dryly, 'but we might improve, given the right encouragement.'

Eden didn't feel up to asking him to be more explicit. As his eyes rested briefly on her lips, her skin prickled uncomfortably. Without meaning to, she said in a low voice, 'You know my parents are divorced?'

Unexpectedly he put out a hand to take hold of hers gently. 'I remember your mother, Eden, and I didn't mean to remind you of her, this evening. This is what comes of expressing an idle thought. More often than not one goes too far and someone gets hurt.'

'Oh, I'm not feeling hurt,' Eden hastened to assure him, loving the comfort she was somehow deriving from his steely fingers, knowing that if she had been upset his tender touch would soon have soothed her. 'I don't say I approve of what my mother did, but I think I forgave her long ago. I don't know about my father, though.'

'You've seen her since?' He made no comment on Joe.

'Yes, in London. She married again, did you know?'

'I believe someone once told me—perhaps it was Joe. Did she never want you with her?'

'In London, the one time I spoke to her alone, she said I could live with her if I wanted to, but I didn't. Apart from anything else, I thought the climate too cold.'

Vern laughed, as if this both amused and relieved him. 'So the U.K. didn't appeal to you?'

'Not really.'

'Yet both your parents are English.'

'Yes . . .' Eden stared at the dashboard unseeingly. That was true, but Joe's grandfather had come to Jamaica when he was young and fallen in love with it. He had settled, in the same house where Joe and she lived now, after marrying a local girl. On the other hand, his son, Joe's father, had gone to England to study law and never come back. Joe had been brought up in London but, as a struggling artist, had been regarded as a bit of a reprobate by disapproving parents. When his grandfather had died, naming Joe his sole heir, he had been glad to come here to get away from them. He had brought his young wife with him, already several months pregnant, but she had never been happy in the lonely house in one of the most isolated coves on the island. When Eden was only a few years old she had returned to England, leaving her baby and a note for Joe saying she would divorce him.

A sigh escaped Eden as she looked up and caught Vern reading her transparent face. 'I guess I like the West Indies,' she said lamely. 'After all, I was born here.'

'It's as good a place as any to be,' he agreed softly. 'Jamaica is the third largest island in the Caribbean and, despite rumours to the contrary, I believe it has a lot going for it.'

Over a very late dinner in Montego Bay, at a night-club she felt no one could have chosen better, she found the courage to ask him, 'You seem to like Jamaica almost as much as Joe, so why do you spend as much time in America?'

He answered with skilful evasion, she thought. 'The last time I was here you and Joe were away. That must have been when you were in London.'

'Yes,' she nodded, 'we were there six months. Someone Joe knew persuaded him to give an exhibition, but it wasn't a great success. Neither was our trip. It was cold and we couldn't afford much in the way of lodgings.'

Vern's hard mouth tightened. 'Why wasn't the exhibition a success?'

Eden forgot he hadn't answered her question. 'I'm not sure.' Her bluey-grey eyes darkened unhappily. 'I think Joe has lost—well,' she hesitated, 'I heard one critic referring to it as his former magic, while another said he had lost his aggressiveness, whatever that means.'

Vern nodded, as if he understood. 'Why do you think this should be?'

'I don't know. He once told me that to be a good artist you have to have a strong desire to communicate your ideas and what you see. I think he must have lost the desire to really communicate with anyone after my mother left him.'

Vern didn't seem overly impressed and she guessed, having heard some of his views on women, that he would never allow one of them to influence his life to this extent. But then all men didn't have his apparent strength of character. The food was superb; she ate delicious lobster tails and fresh pineapple and attempted to guess what was in the sauce, rather than concentrate on the strong lines of Vern's face, but after a few minutes she gave up trying.

In the lengthening silence, she heard Vern asking,

'Do you take after your father in any way? Have you inherited his artistic ability? He was once quite famous.'

It was nice of Vern to say so. 'Not really.' She laid down her fork and knife carefully. 'I did think of going in for three-dimensional design, but to study properly and make a career of it would mean leaving Joe for long spells.'

'So you've given up the idea?'

'No, not entirely,' she smiled, going on to tell him about her painted shells and shell jewellery. 'I'd love to work with silver or ceramics, but at the moment I'm trying to be content with what I can find.'

'Do you ever sell anything?'

'Oh, yes,' Eden's small face lit up eagerly, 'there's a gallery in Montego Bay, run by someone called Fay Derwent. She takes whatever I bring her and she says it sells very well.'

'I know her.'

Eden supposed he might as Fay had lived here most of her life, as Vern had. Jamaica was a large island, almost a hundred and fifty miles long by fifty wide, but it would be unlikely that they had never met. Which brought her back to the question he hadn't answered. As this occurred to her, she forgot about her shells.

'You still haven't told me why you spend so much time in the States.'

'Trying to restore the family fortunes,' he replied lightly, though he didn't look terribly amused. Without elucidating further, he added, 'I hope to come back here permanently, one day.'

'How long do you intend staying this time?' she asked, and waited with a bewildering sense of anxiety for his reply.

'A week or two, it all depends.'

He didn't say what on. As he spoke he stared at Eden narrowly and she couldn't be sure, from his expression, whether he was thinking of her or not.

Realising that the length of his stay wouldn't be influenced by her in any way made her feel unaccountably despondent. Seeing her face fall, Vern suggested gently that she had some more champagne.

'Come on,' he coaxed. 'It's Miguel's best vintage, especially in your honour.' His green eyes gleamed with quick humour. 'It must have been your pretty face, because I can seldom persuade him to produce it.'

Eden suspected Vern might be able to persuade most people to do anything if he really set his mind to it, but she didn't say anything. The champagne, even to her unsophisticated palate, tasted wonderful, but she wasn't sure that she hadn't already drunk too much of it. Miguel, the man who owned the night-club and restaurant, was someone whom Vern appeared to know very well, and, after introducing her, he had told Miguel it was her birthday. He hadn't said which one, but Miguel must have considered her young enough to permit him to ask.

'Ah, a wonderful age, *señorita*,' he had beamed, when she confessed to being eighteen. 'We must certainly help you to make the most of it.' Still exclaiming happily, he had led the way to one of his best tables.

As Eden regarded her empty glass uncertainly, Vern firmly refilled it. 'You've had champagne before?'

She hadn't thought he was watching her closely enough to notice her looking doubtful. Smiling rather selfconsciously, she admitted she had. 'But nothing as potent as this.'

He grinned. 'I'm not trying to get you drunk. I promise to see you home safely.'

Apprehensively, not altogether reassured, Eden blinked at him. 'It's what could happen before then.'

He laughed, his eyes regarding her anxious ones with amusement. 'You aren't suggesting I might try and seduce you, young Eden?'

She went scarlet and to hide the disturbed feeling that

rushed over her, replied indignantly, 'I wish you wouldn't keep calling me that, every time you say my name. I'm not all that young!'

His mouth twisted wryly. 'Perhaps I have to convince myself you are.'

'Why?'

He laughed again, but gently. 'No one but one so young and innocent would ask that.'

Eden watched the bubbles in her champagne with too much interest to be convincing. 'You make it sound as if you believe I should still be in my cradle!'

Instantly he sobered, scrutinising her intently. 'You're very young, Eden. At least you seem so to me, eighteen to my thirty-three. And I suspect, in experience, you're even younger than your years. So don't tempt me, honey.'

Still she felt unsatisfied. 'You did say you thought me old enough to be married!'

'You're very nubile,' he admitted.

'So,' she retorted, with a little wine induced bravado and resentment, 'what is this experience you talk of? Surely it amounts to little more than a few kisses?'

'Which just proves how young you are.' His eyes deliberately levelled on the tender curves of her breasts. 'There's a lot more to it than merely a few chaste kisses, as you will one day undoubtedly find out.'

The champagne had gone to her head. She had thought it was going in the opposite direction, but she wasn't worrying about it now, not when the world had taken on such a rosy hue and she was feeling so gloriously reckless. Meeting his darkly considering glance, she smiled brightly. 'I'll have to begin some time—somewhere.'

'But not with me!' His glance hardened again as it swept over her. 'You have all the makings of a little tease, Eden, but I have no desire—perhaps intention might be a more appropriate word, of initiating you into the delights of making love. And a man of my age is seldom content with a few kisses.'

'Why don't you say naïve kisses and be done with it?' Eden flushed as her mood swung sharply.

Vern looked really angry for a moment, then suddenly relaxed. 'Isn't that the champagne talking?'

Eden stared at him, the challenging light dying out of her eyes as she immediately felt a flicker of shame. Heavily she dropped her head. 'I don't know what got into me . . .' she whispered.

'I told you—the champagne.' Vern leant across the narrow, candlelit table to raise her chin with his index finger, so she could see the forgiving warmth in his eyes. 'It must be partly my fault for giving you so much, but let's not spoil a pleasant evening by quarrelling with each other. Would you like to dance?'

Eden enjoyed the remainder of the evening very much, although she felt guilty over forgetting the time and being late getting home. It was the first time she had been to a night-club, or indeed any kind of organised dance. All the dancing she had done had been in the privacy of their living-room, on her own, after Joe had gone to bed. Sometimes she played tapes and executed a few energy releasing steps with more grace than expertise.

When she confessed to Vern that she couldn't dance properly, he told her there were few people in the West Indies who didn't have some kind of natural rhythm in their blood. This proved to be true, in Eden's case, and after only a few minutes she had mastered her initial awkwardness and was following his more intricate movements effortlessly. But if she enjoyed having him teach her, she enjoyed the sensation of being in his arms even more. Somehow she couldn't help feeling that his strong, resilient body was, in some way a part of her own. Recalling his recent lecture, she didn't say anything, though, especially when such thoughts didn't seem to make sense, not even to herself!

After driving her home and seeing her to her door, Vern informed her that he would be around the following afternoon to have a word with her father.

'Will you be here?' he asked, seeming slightly surprised by his own question.

She nodded, 'But I'll probably be out collecting shells.'

'Okay,' he smiled slightly, 'so I might see you then.'

Suddenly, swiftly, he bent down to touch her lips with his. It was such a feather-light kiss that she almost didn't feel it, but the pleasure which surged through her was real enough. Eden heard herself gasp as Vern whispered huskily, 'I hope you'll consider that as a birthday present until I come back.'

She tried to speak, but before she could find her voice he had turned abruptly in the darkness and left her.

Joe had little to say regarding Eden's night out, next morning.

'If you'd reminded me that it was your birthday, I could have taken you out to dinner.'

Eden allowed him to look reproachful, rather than remark that as he hadn't done any real painting since they had returned from England, they probably couldn't have afforded to go out for anything!

'Vern's coming to see you some time today,' she told him instead. 'At least, that's what he said.'

Indifferently Joe shrugged his shoulders. In his middle fifties, he managed to look ten years older. 'Did you say he was searching for missing tourists when he came across you?'

'Yes,' Eden had already explained. 'I thought it was nice of him to be so concerned.'

'Humph!' Joe grunted, seemingly unimpressed. 'If that's all he was interested in?'

'Well, it wasn't me!' Impatient that she flushed, Eden

replied sharply, 'we barely recognised each other. I'd scarcely been to the plantation until Jessie invited me recently, and I think I've only seen Vern about half a dozen times in my life.'

'When he's been here to see me?'

Eden nodded. 'Sometimes I was out on the beach and only caught an odd glimpse of him. Why does he come here, anyway? I never knew you were friends.'

'Checking up,' Joe said laconically.

'Who is? Whatever do you mean?' Eden asked uncertainly.

'Never mind.' Joe attacked his toast truculently, obviously regretting his brief statement and in no mood to enlighten her.

Anxiously Eden tried to work it out for herself as, with Joe, she so often had to do. Vern's land bordered their own—not that her father's paltry two acres, mostly of shoreline, could be compared with Vern's large plantation, but he must check the boundaries. Of course there was the road in between, but that was what Joe must mean. And while Vern was seeing, after his long absence, that everything was all right, it was only to be expected that he might call and see his neighbour.

The mystery solved, at least to her partial satisfaction, Eden spent an hour going quickly over the house. Joe, having finished his breakfast, stretched lazily, but he did do the washing up before retiring to the porch with the bundle of newspapers which Eden had collected yesterday when she had gone to deliver her latest consignment of shells to Fay Derwent. He would probably sit there until it was time for lunch. He might even have a few sandwiches cut or soup heated when she came in from the beach or the small outhouse where she often worked. On his good days he would sometimes come to meet her, if she had been out on the reefs, and ask if she had found anything interesting. If she had found anything which took his attention, he would examine it and discuss it with her, but while Eden loved him and appreciated his interest, she would rather he had shown more in his own work.

She painted all morning. She was by no means a brilliant artist, but her brushwork was fine and sensitive, and she had picked up a lot from her father, simply by watching him. Usually she only polished her shells. She preferred them this way herself, completely unadorned, just as they came out of the ocean, but on the bottom of some, especially the giant ones, she sometimes did tiny postage-stamp miniatures of typical local scenes. Fay said tourists loved palm trees on white beaches or yachts sailing on blue seas. Occasionally Eden would simply write, in incredibly small, artistic letters, the name of Jamaica or Montego Bay, or Kingston, which was the capital. Lately, though she hadn't told Joe, she had been trying her hand at a few slightly larger landscapes on canvas, which she hoped Fay might like.

After lunch Eden put on her snorkelling equipment and swam out to the reef. In her mask and flippers she dived happily in the clear, warm water, content to watch the huge variety of colourful marine life for a long time before beginning to do any work. The reefs, many of them very near the shore, were always a source of wonder to her and she spent many hours exploring them.

When she did begin looking for suitable shells, she put more effort than she usually did into it. Suddenly it seemed important that she kept as busy as possible so as to prevent herself from thinking of Vern Lomax and their evening out. He had been kind, taking pity on a girl who had had a disappointing day. It would be unwise to read more into his invitation than that, or to exaggerate the funny little stabs of feeling which had gone through her several times during the evening when he had touched her. It would be equally foolish to read anything into his goodnight kiss. It had merely been a brief salute, such as he might have given any girl on her birthday. It might be better to remember, if she remembered anything, that she had twice forgotten to mention his sister. Eden frowned as she avoided a jagged piece of coral. Could it be because she still felt inexplicably uneasy about Jessie's friendship that she was so tardy in laying claim to it?

When she finally waded ashore, Vern was waiting for her. Involuntarily she put a hand over her heart for fear he should notice its suddenly erratic beat. Wearing only a bikini, Eden was doubtful if there was anything to hide the almost racing acceleration of her pulses. She was young and fit, not even the most strenuous exercise affected her so easily, and she stared wide-eyed at the man walking towards her.

'Vern?' she whispered shyly as he paused beside her, and immediately her legs went unaccountably weak.

'Hello, Eden.' Putting out a hand, he laid it gently on her wet hair. 'No need to ask what you've been doing!'

She smiled. It seemed the most she could manage.

His narrowed gaze slid slowly down over her slender, tanned figure and returned to linger closely on her softly tremulous mouth. 'You remind me of a beautiful and very enticing water-nymph,' he said, letting his hand drop to his side again.

The previous evening, when she had been with him, Eden had experienced some rather frightening and bewildering feelings which, in the light of day, she was sure she must have imagined. To find that it was not imagination, that he really did evoke such feelings within her, made her doubly apprehensive. Nervously she tried to tell herself to be careful, to remember he was older and therefore more experienced, but, as she met the searching depth of his intent green eyes she found it difficult to subdue an inner glow of excitement.

'Are you here to see Joe?' she asked at last, trying to speak coolly.

'I've seen Joe.' His eyes caught the flush which stained the apricot smoothness of her cheeks and he smiled gravely. 'I've been looking for you for the past ten minutes. I was beginning to get anxious. What have you been doing, apart from raising my blood pressure?'

'Oh,' she laughed, feeling suddenly more relaxed, 'nothing much. I'm afraid,' she confessed. 'I didn't find anything, at least nothing worth bothering about. One could say I've had a wasted afternoon.'

He ignored this. 'I've been looking at some of your work. I hope you don't mind.'

He was studying her face again, in fact his eyes never seemed to have left it, but she had stopped feeling so selfconscious about it. His opinion of her work was suddenly far more important. 'I—I don't mind in the least,' she stammered. 'What did you think?'

'I like it.' He took hold of her arm, turning her so that they walked up the beach together. Before reaching the house he drew her into the shade of a giant palm. 'I like the kind of hallmark you put on your shells. It's rather distinctive.'

'It seems to make them sell,' she admitted, 'but I prefer them just as they are.'

Vern watched her a little while, his thumb caressing the bare skin of her inner arm, sending delicious little quivers right through her. 'Your small sketches are good too. You appear to have a feeling for colour which is quite remarkable.'

'Perhaps it's that which sometimes makes my work seem better than it actually is,' she replied ruefully.

He brushed such humility aside. 'I think, with proper training, you could have done well at design. Some manufacturer of exclusive fabrics would almost certainly have snapped you up. You could be wasted here.'

Smiling, she shook her head, amazed that he should think so. 'I think I might be happier as I am. This is my home and I'm quite content. Few people ever come here and no developer appears to have discovered it yet. I hope they never will!'

Vern grinned at her slightly fiercer tones. 'So do I.'

'Are you going home now?' she breathed, as their eyes met and they seemed suddenly to be suspended in a world of their own. Immediately she forgot some improbable hotel company whom she might never see.

'Not yet.' As if she had suddenly reminded him of something, Vern thrust his hand in his pocket, drawing out a small package. As he passed it to her, he said softly, 'This is your birthday present—a day late.'

CHAPTER THREE

EDEN felt both startled and delighted as she gazed at the small package Vern placed in her hands. It was so completely unexpected that momentarily she was at loss for words. She couldn't remember the last time anyone had given her anything. Joe just didn't take any notice of her birthdays or Christmas any more.

She was aware, through surprise and delight, of tears in her eyes and felt ashamed. Presents might be few and far between, but otherwise she had so much. What must Vern be thinking of her! 'Is this really for me?' she whispered, controlling her tears.

'You ask the silliest questions, Eden Rossiter,' he teased gently, as if aware of the emotion she was trying hard to conceal. 'Would I have given it to you if it wasn't?'

'I guess not . . .'

He rubbed a finger lightly over her damp cheek. 'Aren't you going to open it?'

'Yes.' Suddenly, like a child, she couldn't get the wrappings off quickly enough. Inside was a box containing a pair of small earrings. Eden drew a sharp breath as her eyes fell on the tiny clusters of what she imagined were semi-precious stones. Although quite plain they looked fabulous.

'Oh, how beautiful!' she breathed tremulously, raising eyes in which more tears had unconsciously gathered. 'It—it's far too much, though, especially after what you've already done.'

Vern didn't smile. He merely shook his head while removing the box from her trembling hands. 'You've had your ears pierced, I noticed.'

'I had it done in England,' she affirmed, feeling dazed, 'but Joe couldn't afford more than gold stoppers.' Again she insisted, 'You shouldn't have spent so much.'

'Eden!' Vern's smile softened his words. 'You're trying my patience making such a fuss over nothing. I gave you the earrings as much for my own pleasure as yours. Now aren't you going to put them on?' She tried to, but under his watchful eyes her fingers were all thumbs.

'Here, let me.'

Obediently she passed the clips to him, her anxious glance pleading his forgiveness. She felt the touch of his fingers against her ears and neck, her skin unbearably sensitive to his gentle manipulation. Something whirled through her, dancing like segments of living flame.

As she winced, Vern apologised, while not allowing it to alter his concentration, 'Sorry, I didn't realise I was hurting.'

'You aren't,' she assured him, then had to think of some excuse for her agitation. 'I suddenly realised that my father might object to your spending so much money on me.'

'You never give up, do you?' He stepped back to survey his handiwork, his eyes narrowly approving the way in which his gift fitted so well against the neat outlines of her small, proud head. 'I didn't actually spend anything, if you must know. I believe these particular earrings belonged to my grandmother when she was a young girl. I feel sure she would have liked you to have them.'

'You mean they're—sort of family heirlooms?'

Vern laughed outright at her outraged expression. 'Don't look as though things are getting worse and worse, Eden.' His eyes hardened imperceptibly. 'I fear you aren't going to be happy until I tell you they aren't worth much, and aren't something anyone else wants.'

Eden, having immediately thought of Jessie, felt faintly reassured. Althought Jessie might consider Vern had no right to give away anything belonging to her family, her taste lay in much more flamboyant jewellery. Tentatively Eden lifted her hands to the small, glittering studs in her ears. She was sure Jessie wouldn't mind her having these.

'I'm sorry,' she said, feeling happier, and was about to confess that it was Jessie she had been worrying about, and that she knew her, when Vern shrugged and said something which again made Eden forget all about his sister.

'I'm going to Kingston tomorrow. I'd like you to come with me, if you will.'

For a second his words didn't sink in, but when they did her face brightened radiantly. 'Why, I'd love to!' she exclaimed.

Steadily he stared down at her. 'That's one thing I particularly like about you, Eden—you don't pretend.'

'Pretend?' She gazed up at him, her eyes enormous with confusion and excitement.

'That you have another engagement. That you aren't interested. Deliberate ploys used by women to titillate a man's appetite.'

The glow in Eden's eyes faded a little, as this seemed to imply she might be too eager for his company. 'I could have had another engagement,' she said warily.

'Easily,' he agreed, his smile a little taut at her tone. 'You're lovely enough to have plenty of engagements. You told me you hadn't any boy-friends, but perhaps that wasn't entirely the truth.'

'It was—it is,' she confessed, flushing unhappily as she realised this might make Vern believe no one else wanted her.

He noted her hot cheeks teasingly. 'I hope that isn't a sign of guilt?'

'No . . .!'

There was a sudden, short silence as he continued to study her, the mockery dying out of his face. For a few quiet moments there was only the droning of the humming birds, the shrill song of the kling-kling and the distant sound of the sea.

Then Vern said rather gravely, 'It's your simplicity, I think.' His hand came out again to touch the earrings he had given her, apparently to adjust them, but when he finished, instead of taking his hand away, he let it curl around her nape. 'Don't get me wrong,' he said softly, as Eden stiffened, 'it's not your intelligence I'm talking about. No one could fault that. It's your aura of complete innocence. I've never come across it before, and it intrigues me.'

Feeling considerably shaken, Eden trembled under his detaining hands. He had placed his other one on her bare shoulder and though he made no attempt to hold her closer, she was wholly conscious of the closeness of his tall, lean body.

When she didn't speak but stared at him a trifle apprehensively, he asked curtly, as if it was suddenly important to him, 'Eden, do you trust me?'

'Of course. Yes, I do!' As she realised how much, she replied emphatically, while a faint bewilderment stole into her eyes. 'Is there any reason why I shouldn't?'

Vern smiled thinly. 'Maybe that's not a question you should be asking a man of my age, honey, but no, as far as you're concerned, there isn't. Now I must be going.'

Swiftly, before she could reply or move, his hand tightened on her neck to hold her head still as he bent and kissed her. He was a little more thorough than he had been the night before, but not overly so. Eden felt the sting of his lips as he brushed them over her quivering mouth, then she was free.

'See you in the morning, early,' he said as he moved away.

It wasn't until he had disappeared out of sight that

Eden remembered she hadn't thanked him properly for her birthday present.

The next day was the first of a series of such days which Vern and Eden spent together. For Eden time seemed to have taken on a kind of new enchantment. Vern took her out several times, but seemed determined that they should get to know each other slowly. He not only asked her out but he talked to her a lot as well, until it seemed to Eden that even their thoughts were compatible.

He never mentioned going back to the States and she didn't ask, for suddenly she couldn't bear to think of him going away again. Joe had little to say regarding the number of times she went out with Vern, or the increasing frequency of his visits. Eden suspected that he believed the day would soon come when Vern would leave and that might be the last they would see of him. There was certainly nothing in his manner to suggest he took their friendship seriously.

Eden eventually found an opportunity to tell Vern that she knew his sister, and how she considered Jessie had once saved her life. She had been exploring some caves, on a rocky part of the coast only accessible from the sea, when she discovered that the dinghy, with the outboard motor she had used to reach them, had cut adrift. If Jessie hadn't arrived in her small motorboat, an hour later, she didn't know what she would have done.

'Drowned, for sure,' she had said lightly, and had been surprised to see how pale Vern had gone under his tan. 'Jessie wasn't in any danger,' she had added quickly, thinking that must be the reason for his sudden grimness.

'It's not Jessie I'm worried about,' he had returned curtly. 'What happened to your dinghy? Did you ever find it again?'

'Yes, washed up, completely wrecked,' she had

confessed ruefully. 'We don't have anything now, and I miss it.'

'Good!' Vern had exclaimed, so harshly that she had been puzzled.

This afternoon she was getting ready to visit his plantation. He had asked her to go early and stay for dinner. Joe had been asked too, but he had declined.

'I'm getting too old for gadding about,' he had excused himself. 'I've reached the age when I'd rather stay at home.'

Eden hadn't tried to persuade him. If Joe was determined to become a recluse there was little she could do about it. She felt hurt that he hadn't accepted Vern's invitation, but she didn't think Vern would mind all that much. He appeared to know Joe almost as well as she did.

It was four when Vern arrived to pick her up, and she heard him talking to Joe on the porch. She had changed into fresh shorts and another shirt, but she still had only her pink dress to wear later. Rather unhappily she packed it in a small carrier, hoping Vern wouldn't notice how often she had worn it.

'Ready?' He glanced around with a smile when she appeared, reaching out a long arm to pull her to him and kiss her gently. She could see this rather startled Joe, who glanced at them sharply.

Her face was very flushed as Vern bundled her, a little less gently, into his car. 'Don't push me!' she cried angrily. 'I'm quite capable of getting in by myself!'

Looking as angry as she was, he snapped, 'If you can't bear me touching you just say so!'

Suddenly, as they roared off, the anger drained from her. 'It wasn't that, Vern, and you know it. It was just what Joe might think,' she tried to explain, in some confusion. 'I don't want him worrying about me and reading me a lecture. Once he gets something in his head, he's apt to go on and on about it.'

'Why should he worry about you?'

'Oh,' her flush deepened miserably, as she stuttered and stammered, 'he—well, he might be frightened you led me a-astray.'

Vern laughed unkindly. 'It mightn't be very difficult. It might easily happen one day, as I believe I've already told you.'

'Stop it!' she whispered, feeling as bruised as if he had hit her. 'You know how to hurt when you want to!'

'I'd like to . . .!' Suddenly he paused, his white knuckles relaxing on the steering-wheel. Amusement edged his voice as he asked, 'Can you tell me what we're arguing about, Eden? I'm sorry, honey.'

Eden had no hesitation in allowing her hand to creep into the one he held out. 'I'm sorry too,' she responded fervently.

They were both laughing, as he teased her back to a happier frame of mind, when they reached Vern's home, about four miles away. He lived in an old plantation house, huge and rambling, reached along a winding drive bordered by a forest of trees. Over the drive, bamboo formed a veritable cathedral and behind them stood breadfruit and banyan trees with royal palm and many-hued hibiscus, to name just a few that Eden could see.

The interior of the house was not outstandingly stylish, but it was comfortable. As they entered, Vern glanced round with a frown.

'Jessie came a couple of months before me to supervise some decorating, but she doesn't appear to have achieved much, so far. She wants to stay on.'

Eden didn't reply. She didn't believe the house was the reason why Jessie wanted to stay on. If Jessie was reluctant to return to the States, Eden thought it was more likely to be because of Diego Dexter. Eden knew they were good friends, if not lovers. Having seen them together, she suspected the latter, and knew instinctively that Vern wouldn't approve. She wasn't sure that she did herself. Diego might be good-looking, and good at his job, but, as a man, she didn't like him. She always had a feeling that he was far from trustworthy.

'Where is Jessie?' she asked lightly, as Vern ushered her over the large hall into the equally spacious drawing-room.

He pushed her down gently on one of the comfortable sofas and rang for tea. 'She's out, I'm afraid.' He didn't look altogether sorry. 'Some friends rang this morning, inviting her to visit for a couple of days. I hope you don't mind her being away? She did actually offer to stay when I told her you were coming.'

'No, I don't mind,' Eden replied quite truthfully. She would rather be alone with Vern, without Jessie's disparaging eye on them all the time, although she immediately felt appalled for having thought of such a thing. She couldn't help wondering, though, what Jessie had thought about Vern bringing her here. Somehow she couldn't believe Jessie would like it?

A big Jamaican woman, whom Eden had met before, brought their tea. Mrs Prince beamed at her, because they had taken to each other immediately, and they chatted together for several minutes while Vern listened sardonically.

'You get on well with everyone, don't you?' he commented, when Mrs Prince had gone.

'Any reason why I shouldn't?' she asked gravely.

'None,' he replied quietly. 'But Jessie is much older than you and she doesn't. She always seems to have had this difficulty.'

Eden knew what he meant but didn't say anything. She might have said this was Jessie's own fault. She was too fond, Eden had discovered, of looking for the weak points in others and poking fun at them—even exploiting them. She also liked having her own way and she definitely imagined she was vastly superior to the people who worked on the estate. Yet she must have good qualities, Eden reasoned, or Vern wouldn't be so fond of her. And, she reminded herself, hadn't Jessie practically saved her life? She couldn't repay her by openly criticising her!

Vern drank his tea and watched her idly. He didn't say anything more about his sister and seemed to be thinking of something else instead. Just when she was beginning to wonder if there was a smut on her nose, he suggested they spent the whole of the next day sailing.

She sighed, knowing there was nothing she would like better. 'I'd love to, Vern, but I have work to do. Joe and I have to live.'

'Why not let him do his share for a change?' Vern asked cynically.

'You know why,' she murmured unhappily.

'Yes.' His mouth clamped, obviously on other things he would liked to have said. Then he shrugged. 'One or two days aren't going to make any difference.'

'No, all right,' she smiled, weakly giving in. Her smile disappeared as she realised he meant she would have plenty of time once he returned to the States.

Later they went for a swim. Eden hadn't brought her bikini, but Vern said she could borrow one of Jessie's. As Jessie must be at least two sizes bigger, Eden felt dubious, but Vern didn't give her time to protest.

On their way to the pool, towards which he guided her swiftly, they bumped into his plantation manager. Vern spoke to him curtly without stopping, but Diego paused long enough to smile at Eden warmly. 'Hello, Eden,' he said.

'Hello,' she replied stiffly, aware of Vern's suddenly narrowed eyes.

'I didn't know you were so well acquainted,' he said coldly, as Diego walked on.

'I scarcely know him!' she retorted.

It was Vern's sceptical glance that brought a flush to

her cheeks, but he clearly mistook it for guilt. His eyes hardened as he rasped, 'Dexter's a good enough manager, Eden, but he's not the sort I'd like a girl like you to be too friendly with. Don't tell me you fancy him?'

Unhappily Eden shook her head, hoping that would convince him. She found it impossible to tell him that it was his sister, not herself, who was fond of Diego. It should have been easy to mention this casually, but somehow Eden found she couldn't. Some instinct warned her that if she did Jessie would never forgive her. And she had no means of knowing for certain just how far Jessie was involved with Diego. She could have been mistaken about them.

The pool, set a little distance from the house, was large but had an air of neglect about it.

'My mother had it laid out a few years before she and my father died,' Vern told Eden. 'Have you been here before?'

'No.' He didn't seem to want her sympathy because of his parents and she didn't offer any, although, looking at the pool and the beauty of the surrounding gardens, she couldn't help feeling sad that they hadn't lived to enjoy it longer. 'Jessie asked me for tea, but we didn't come here.'

'Did she show you over the house?'

Because Vern's tone was terse, Eden replied quickly, 'No, but it doesn't matter. I came for tea, not a guided tour. She probably didn't think I'd be interested.'

'I'll show you later,' he said curtly.

As she went to one of the changing rooms, where he said she would find a spare bikini. Eden wondered why he was so insistent. Surely it couldn't matter to him whether she saw over the house or not? To herself, she confessed she would like to, but she didn't want him to realise how important everything about him—and concerning him—was becoming to her.

Slowly she slipped out of her shorts and pulled on one of the several bikinis she found hanging in a cupboard. As she had feared, both the bra and briefs were on the big side and she had some trouble in adjusting them before going to join Vern in the pool.

He was waiting for her, his wet hair and invigorated expression a clear indication that he had already swam several lengths. Eden tried not to look too closely at his bare shoulders and broad chest as he reached out of the water to take her hand and draw her in from where she hesitated on the tiled edge. She hoped he would imagine her racing pulse was due to nervousness, but as she shyly met his teasing eyes, she couldn't be sure.

Afterwards they lay on padded loungers in the sun and dried off. Swimming in the pool had cooled the heat from Eden's body but done nothing to steady her pulse. She had seen Vern in brief trunks before, for he often swam with her, these days, among the reefs, but somehow, this afternoon, the sight of him with so little on was affecting her oddly. She found it difficult to tear her eyes from his tall, muscled frame. He had a big but perfectly proportioned body, his broad shoulders tapering to a lean but substantial waist and powerfully curved buttocks.

He had his eyes closed and for a moment she took advantage of this to allow her glance to linger on his dark, rugged face. He might not be strictly good-looking, but his features held a stength and charm which she suspected few women might resist.

When she began to wonder what it would be like to creep on the lounger beside him, she clamped down on her wayward thoughts. After swallowing several times to ease a peculiar tightness in her throat, she managed to ask idly, 'You have a big plantation here, Vern. What do you grow?'

Barely turning his head, Vern slanted a measured glance at her but answered in the same tone.

'Sugar cane, bananas and coconut with coffee higher up.'

'It's a wonder you don't have to be here all the time.' She watched an insect settle lightly on one of her legs. 'It sounds as if there's a lot to do.'

'A lot of scope for doing more, I think.' Deftly he leant over to flip the fly off her slender limb.

The touch of his hand brought back a growing desire to be in his arms, to feel their scantily clad bodies close to each other. With an effort she kept her mind on the conversation she had started with such determination.

'There's still a lot of sugar in Jamaica.'

'It's still a major crop, but thank goodness we don't have slaves any more. Jamaica has come a long way since them, though. We're now the largest producer of bauxite in the world, I have an interest in it myself, and tourism brings in a lot of foreign income.

Eden liked the way he spoke as if he still considered Jamaica his country. She turned her back, happier that her bikini seemed to have shrunk a little as it dried and now covered her better. Once or twice in the pool she had thought she was going to lose it. Above her head, the branches of massive tropical trees were still in the heat of the afternoon. Even the butterflies and birds appeared to be drowsing.

'It's funny,' she mused thoughtfully, 'I've lived in Jamaica all my life, yet I haven't seen much of it.'

'I'm enjoying showing it to you,' Vern smiled. 'You won't be able to say that much longer.'

She laughed. 'I wasn't hinting. Besides, I've work to do. After tomorrow,' she said firmly, 'I'll really have to get stuck in.'

He laughed at her expression and with a swift, agile movement suddenly left his lounger to sit beside her. Ruthlessly he pushed her over and she could feel the weight of him pressing against her. 'What you really need,' he said, 'is someone to look after you.'

Meeting his smiling yet intent glance, she felt startled. 'I have Joe.'

'I rather think it's you who's trying to look after him.' When she didn't reply he grew silent, staring down into her wide eyes, then, with a soft exclamation, he pulled her up against him and began kissing her.

This was the first time he had kissed her properly, and though Eden had felt mysteriously frustrated by his former, feather-light caresses, she wasn't prepared for the surge of feeling which went through her now. He seemed for a moment to forget all about being gentle, and as his mouth bruised hers she felt suddenly frightened by something she didn't entirely understand. It was as if all her innocence was making one last stand against wanton forces within her striving for control— forces such as she had never realised she possessed before.

Vern's long, sensuous kisses were sending shivers of exquisite delight all over her body, but she fought against the encroaching languor this induced. When her arms would have wound round his neck, she gripped the sides of the lounger frantically to stop them and deliberately tightened her lips.

As if suddenly conscious of her silent resistance, Vern slowly raised his head. 'Eden,' he muttered huskily, 'is something wrong? Am I frightening you?'

How could she tell him she was more frightened of herself, of the strange, unfamiliar desires sweeping through her which she dared not give in to. Nodding coldly, she said stormily, 'Yes, you are! I'm not used to being mauled.'

The glint of anger in his eyes almost shrivelled her. 'I wasn't mauling you,' he exclaimed. 'And you can't deny you wanted me to kiss you. You've been throwing out signals all afternoon. Was I supposed to ignore them?'

'You're mistaken!' Flushing with shame, she glared back at him, wondering how she had ever come to think she liked him. 'I'd like to go home, if you don't mind. If you wouldn't mind getting off me!'

He didn't move. He merely laughed harshly, which convinced her he was still angry. 'You aren't going anywhere until we've sorted this out. I still say you wanted me to kiss you, and if you've had enough—well, I haven't. I'm not nearly satisfied.'

His arms tightened relentlessly about her and as she twisted frantically he held her firmly so she couldn't evade his descending mouth. She tried to continue fighting him, but the pressure of his lips and the movements of his hands over her bare skin were rapidly draining the strength from her. As a fire kindled in her blood, her resistance diminished and soon she was clinging to him, her response everything he might have wished for.

This time, when he caressed her warm, slender body, she quivered with pleasure rather than fear, and when he kissed her again and again, she arched instinctively against him and didn't try to prevent her arms from going round his neck.

Just as they did so, however, he paused, looking down at her, breathing unevenly, his eyes so dark with desire that she immediately felt afraid again.

'Vern, please,' she breathed, her voice pleading now instead of angry.

The expression in his eyes at once changed to one of smouldering tenderness. 'Darling, I didn't mean to harm you.'

Unhappily she shook her head. 'I'm sorry,' she whispered.

'You're so innocent,' he groaned, his fingers threading gently through her long, lustrous hair which spread out on the pillow behind her. 'Sometimes,' he confessed thickly, 'I wish you were more experienced.'

'I'm sorry,' she repeated, tears suddenly on her cheeks, 'I don't suppose you want to see me again . . .'

He kissed away her tears, his eyes warm, his mouth tender. 'Don't be foolish, honey. Of course I want to see you again.'

'You just said,' she reminded him in a strangled voice, 'you wished I'd had more experience.'

The lines of his face hardened slightly, but his eyes were still tender. 'I want you, you must know that. One day I mean to have you. I don't want to frighten you, but perhaps it's only right that I should give you fair warning.'

Eden lay perfectly still in his arms, knowing suddenly that she wanted him. If, as yet, she was unable to put it in words as easily as he did, there could be no mistaking such a feeling of overwhelming desire.

She shivered, although there was still much heat left in the afternoon. She wanted to belong to Vern completely, but in return she might want more than he was prepared to offer. He hadn't said that he loved her, she didn't know if she loved him, and she suddenly knew she could never give herself to any man until she was sure that they loved each other. This was what she had to have time to think about, what she couldn't explain.

Vern, more aware of her tumultuous thoughts than she realised, spoke softly. 'You wouldn't regret giving yourself to me, Eden. I think I could satisfy all your needs.'

'I—I'd have to think about it,' she whispered.

'Take as long as you want.' He let his hands slide slowly up her thin arms to her creamy shoulders, his thumbs searching and massaging tender hollows on the way, then abruptly he stood up, as though he couldn't trust his control any further, and dived swiftly into the pool.

Later, Eden changed into her pink dress and they dined together in the softly lit dining-room of Vern's home. The meal Mrs Prince served them was superb, but Eden found she had little appetite. As they ate, Vern talked lightly of the island and its people, their future role in world affairs, and while Eden appreciated that he was trying to help her relax, she found it difficult. Her thoughts were too chaotic. Since the interlude by the pool, when he had shown her how much he wanted her, she had felt quite different from the young girl she had been a few hours ago. Then she had been almost a child. Now, she knew without a shadow of doubt that she was a woman. Vern might not have violated her innocence, but otherwise he had managed to change her completely.

That was as far as she allowed herself to go. Vern wasn't pressing her at all. He was being kind, entertaining her, giving her a wonderful dinner. It would be poor compensation, to say nothing of bad manners, if she sat like a robot all evening! When she returned home there would be time enough to sort out her feelings.

Making an effort, she began chatting brightly. She even managed to laugh over her pink dress. 'You must be tired of seeing it,' she declared.

Vern put out a hand towards hers across the table. He often did this when she was with him and usually, unable to resist, she placed her hand trustingly in his. Tonight, for the first time, she felt terribly nervous about it.

When a lightning-like sensation shot up her arm, she knew she had been right to be apprehensive. But before she could withdraw, he said tenderly. 'You'd look beautiful in anything, Eden. I never notice what you're wearing. Other women might have more expensive clothes, but they don't have your beauty or innocence.'

As their eyes met, a warm feeling of being cared for and protected flowed over her, a feeling that was still with her much later, as Vern showed her over the house.

'We ought to have done this when you arrived,' he smiled, switching on lights as they wandered upstairs. 'At least the darkness might hide some shabby corners.'

Vern's home might look as if it could do with a lick of paint in places, but it wasn't nearly as shabby as her own. Eden sighed with envy rather than in agreement as she followed him around.

'I love it,' she said. 'It's wonderful.' And he grinned and replied that he would sooner she thought this of him than his house.

His teasing mood continued until they reached his own quarters, 'What do you think?' he asked, watching her closely as he threw open his bedroom door.

Like all the other rooms they had visited, Vern's room was huge, and although he had been away, the stamp of his dominant personality still seemed on it. Eden's mouth went dry as she looked around. It was so utterly masculine it couldn't have belonged to anyone but him.

Because the feelings she thought she had under control were returning to taunt her, she forced herself to reply carelessly, 'What do your other girl-friends think?'

His mouth tightened as he paid her back in her own coin. 'I've never asked them. There hasn't always been time.'

Eden gazed at the wide bed with hurt eyes. That could mean many things, and no doubt she deserved the pain of the thoughts he thrust so cruelly on her. He meant her to wonder if he had been in too great a hurry to make love to these other women to ask their opinion of the room they were in.

'I shouldn't have said that, should I?' she whispered miserably.

At the sight of the sudden tears in her eyes, with a thick exclamation Vern reached out swiftly to draw her to him.

'Oh, Eden, my little love, I'm sorry! It wasn't anything so very bad, but I've got a hell of a temper.'

As he had done by the pool, he kissed away her tears and she began unconsciously clinging to him. 'Forgive me,' he muttered.

She was too content to be in his arms to do anything else. 'Of course,' she sighed tremulously, hugging him tightly.

The quality of his kisses changed, as if the feel of her slight body trembling against his aroused him inexplicably. 'I've never had another woman in here, or in that bed,' he said huskily, 'but I'd give all I've got to have you.'

As he pressed rough kisses on her face and mouth Eden felt a sudden wild urge to give in to him. He must care for her a little! She laid her hands on his chest and felt his heart leaping under them. She could almost feel the need and the tension within him, the passion surging through his lean body.

'Vern?' she breathed, raising her head so she could look at him, her eyes wide and slightly dazed but not trying to hide any more, or make a defence of her own immaturity. 'You can have me, if you love me.'

She was unprepared for the dangerous light which flickered over his face. He stopped kissing her and his mouth went grim. 'Are you quoting terms, by any chance, Eden?'

She wasn't sure what he was talking about and her eyes widened. 'No, of course not . . .'

For a long moment he stared at her enigmatically, the muscles of his face taut as he appeared to be holding himself under steely restraint. Then suddenly he sighed deeply and pushed her away.

'I'd rather wait,' he said curtly, 'until you really understand what it is you're offering, and you're ready to come to me unconditionally!'

CHAPTER FOUR

IT was late the following evening when Vern brought her back to the island. They had had a wonderful day, the kind of day, Eden thought wistfully, one wished would never end. Soon it would be over, and she began feeling terribly depressed, although why this should be she had no idea. Nothing lasted for ever and there would be other days, perhaps as full of magic, because she was sure this wouldn't be the last time Vern would ask her out.

Frowning, she searched for his tall figure, but he had popped down below to check something in the cabin and for the moment she was alone. There had been nothing in his attitude all day to suggest that anything was wrong. He had been as attentive as ever, so why should she suddenly feel that dark clouds were gathering on the horizon and that for her the sun might never shine as brightly again?

While she watched the fast approaching coastline she tried to lighten her present mood by concentrating on the past few hours. They had set off early that morning. Vern had a power-boat—the same boat in which she had gone sailing with Jessie and Diego Dexter. It wasn't large, but Eden thought it was beautiful. Jessie had told her there had been a yacht when her parents were alive, but it had been sold. Vern hadn't mentioned it.

Eden knew she would have been content in a rowing boat if Vern was with her. They had sailed a long way and he had shown her several uninhabited islands. They had dropped anchor by one of them and gone ashore for lunch. Vern had built a fire and cooked the fish he had caught earlier. They had been delicious, and afterwards, after they had swum in the blue waters of the bay, she had fallen asleep, only to be wakened later by Vern kissing her.

He had his arms around her and was kissing her gently. 'I resisted as long as I could,' he had smiled, his smile fading as her response, though sleepy, had been warm and immediate.

Eden wasn't very old and hadn't been sure she was ready for a revelation that almost frightened her, but it was then that she had realised she loved him. They had been swimming and not bothered to get dressed, and their almost bare bodies, pressing against each other, had proved unbearably stimulating. Vern's kisses, his hard, caressing hands, had nearly driven her out of her mind. She hadn't been able to prevent herself from offering herself to him again.

Back on board, she had been grateful that he hadn't taken advantage of her clinging arms and feverish words. Once she had had time to return to normal, she had been relieved that Vern's common sense and better control had enabled him to hug her tenderly then put her firmly away from him. Yet she knew now, with cheeks hot again, that she would never have regretted belonging to him completely. Not now that she realised she loved him.

He came up on deck and slowed the boat, as if, he too was in no hurry for the day to end. Coming to where she was sitting, he sat down beside her, slipping an arm round her, pulling her close.

'Happy?'

She was too conscious of the sinewy strength of his body not to tremble, but she managed to smile and assure him she was. She was happy, that was true. If she wanted too much, too soon it was scarcely Vern's fault. Until a few hours ago she hadn't been really sure what she wanted herself. Perhaps she had been over-hasty and the time and place had been wrong? He had said, in his bedroom, that he would wait until she was ready to come to him unconditionally, so it must be something like this.

As though he sensed her despondency and could read her thoughts, his hand curved her long, graceful neck to turn her chin up so he could kiss her tenderly. 'I want you to take your time, Eden. You've very young and it's easy to be too impulsive. At my age one has the experience to make the right decisions, but you haven't. I don't want you committing yourself to something you might regret. I've had time to think, since last night, and I'm sorry if I tried to rush you.'

Vern's new attitude being so much at variance with her present mood, Eden rebelled against it. 'How old do I have to be before you believe I know my own mind?' she asked coldly.

He laughed, pressing light kisses round her softly mutinous mouth. 'How about twenty-five or so? That's always seemed to me to be a sensible age.'

'You can't be serious!' she gasped.

'Don't tempt me,' he replied, all the humour out of his eyes in an instant.

'I'd like to.'

'Braver by the minute!' Removing his mouth from the vicinity of hers, he shook her without using strength. 'I'm willing to give you time, darling. You'd better take it while I'm still in a comparatively sane frame of mind. Considering the effect you have on me, I think it's a pretty generous offer. I've only so much control and it may not last long.'

Being unsure of him in this mood, Eden sighed and dipped her head. Did she have any other option but to take his advice? It was impossible to tell if he felt anything for her, other than a casual desire to sleep with her. And even this, despite what he said, couldn't be overwhelming as he had easily resisted her on the deserted beach.

'Will I see you tomorrow?' she asked anxiously, as he reluctantly dropped his hands from her shoulders and rose to his feet.

'No.' Vern concentrated his attention on guiding the boat through the deep inlet of the rocky cove where he kept it. 'I have to see someone in Kingston. The appointment was made before I left the States. I would have taken you with me, but I expect to be tied up for most of the day and I don't want you wandering about Kingston on your own.'

Darkness was falling as he delivered her back to Joe. Eden, feeling helpless and bewildered out of her depth, suddenly didn't want him to leave her. She had a perhaps foolish but quite desperate urge to detain him at all costs, but he refused her offer of coffee.

His green eyes glinted, she thought for a moment he was going to agree, then he ruefully shook his head. 'I'm sorry, honey. I have some papers to look up for tomorrow. I should have been sorting them out today.'

'Goodnight, then.' She wondered if her cheeks were flushed but didn't much care, as she raised her face, shamelessly begging him to kiss her.

He did yet so gently it did nothing to satisfy the growing hunger within her.

But just as he left, she heard him say roughly, as if against his will, 'I might call tomorrow, on my way home, if I'm not too late.'

Jessie called to see her next morning. Eden, recalling how she had reminded Vern that she had work to do, realised wryly that she might have done better to remind herself. If Vern had asked her to go with him to Kingston, she knew she wouldn't have hesitated.

She was in her workshop, guiltily trying to make up for lost time, when Jessie found her.

'Forgive me,' Jessie knocked lightly on the door and pushed it open, 'but Vern told me what you did and I was curious.'

Smiling, she looked round with interest, and again Eden was puzzled by the uneasiness she always felt when she was with the other girl.

'There's not much to see, I'm afraid.'

'Never mind.' Jessie picked up a beautifully coloured painting of underwater coral and fish and with a slight shrug laid it down again. 'I had nothing else to do. With Vern around, I dare scarcely speak to Diego.'

'Surely,' Eden said carefully, 'you're old enough to please yourself?'

'One would imagine so,' Jessie exclaimed sullenly, 'but you try telling my dear brother that! Unfortunately he holds the purse strings.'

Eden immediately felt indignant on Vern's behalf because of the underlying criticism she clearly detected. 'Vern's very responsible, and he does work hard.'

'Sometimes,' Jessie allowed tartly, 'not always. He's off this morning to the races in Kingston. A certain lady he knows invited him down a few days ago and I thought, as he'll be having a good time, he'd be willing to let the staff take it easy for a change, but no! He's left Diego enough to keep him busy for a week!'

Abruptly Eden began tidying her work-bench, which didn't really need it. Clumsily she knocked over a precious tin of oil, which, as she mopped it up, ironically provided her with a genuine excuse for turning her back on Jessie. Her hands were cold and clammy, a dreadful sickness rose in her throat. She had never felt this way before. Why had Vern lied to her? Of course, she reasoned with herself, Jessie could have made a mistake. She didn't seem very happy this morning, nor did she appear to be aware that Eden and Vern had been seeing a lot of each other. At least this was something! Unconsciously, Eden bit her lip and winced at the pain.

'Your brother might soon be returning to the States,' she said stiffly, still with her back to Jessie, for fear something of the shock she had suffered showed in her face.

'That's one consolation,' Jessie muttered. 'Rona's been ringing him often enough, I don't think he can hold out much longer. He was just saying if he doesn't go back she's liable to come here, and he doesn't want her seeing the place until he gets it smartened up a bit.'

Eden's voice sounded raw when she finally found it. 'Who's—Rona?'

Jessie didn't notice her anguished tones, or that she had suddenly stopped working and gone completely still. 'The girl he's engaged to—well, practically engaged to,' she shrugged, as if it was the same thing. 'They would have been married, Rona told me this herself, if she hadn't had to go to Australia for her cousin's wedding. Vern was furious, I think they almost fell out over it, but from what he was saying, the other night, I gather he still loves her.'

At this point, as the agony which Jessie's unwitting disclosures had aroused attacked her afresh, Eden was jerked from the retrospective daze into which she had fallen. As she realised what had happened, with a stricken moan she rolled over on her stomach and tried to control her turbulent thoughts. Vern's return must have brought everything back, and she didn't want to remember . . .

She tried not to think how, after lunch that day, she had given up all pretext of working, and, without saying anything to Joe, had gone to sit on a high vantage point on the edge of Vern's plantation, from which it was possible to see a network of roads, the one that ran round the island those leading to both Vern's house and her own. She had intended making sure that if he called, as he had said he might do, she wouldn't be in. Apart from breaking her heart, he had made a fool of her, and she couldn't bear to face him.

She tried not to remember Diego Dexter's car coming

from the north, turning at the plantation junction with Jessie sitting beside him. They had passed quite close to where she was sitting and parked in a clearing only a few hundred yards away. Then, like an act from a fast moving and frightening film, she had turned her head in time to see Vern disappearing down her road-end. He had obviously left Kingston early.

Strangely, considering the state she was in, Eden had thought immediately of Jessie. Other people might go straight past but if Vern noticed Diego's parked car he might easily investigate. She could imagine his rage if he caught his sister and Diego together. She had run all the way down the steep hillside to warn Jessie. It seemed little enough to do after Jessie had saved her life.

Without realising it was bitterness driving her she had reached the clearing. Wrenching open the car door, she had surprised Jessie in Diego's arms. They had only been kissing each other, but Jessie had been furiously angry until Eden had explained. Then she hadn't been able to move fast enough, but as she had jumped from her seat in the car, she had turned quickly, catching Eden off balance and pushing her into it.

'You'd better stay there,' she had cried, 'until I get away.'

Eden could still recall how stunned she had been, and that hadn't been the worst of it. Before she could escape, Diego had caught her close, crushing her protesting mouth with his. 'We may as well make a good job of it, for Jessie's sake,' he had muttered mockingly.

Eden still had nightmares, after all this time, of Vern pulling into the clearing behind them. Of being literally torn from Diego's arms while Vern's cold clipped tones had ordered him to report to his office immediately. And, after Diego had gone, of Vern telling her in no uncertain terms exactly what he thought of her. He had called her a tramp, among other, unrepeatable things.

He had plainly stated that he wouldn't be seeing her again, that he was returning to the States in a day or two with his sister.

The dire consequences of her impulsive action hadn't really sunk in until later, and when this happened Eden had been shattered. Yet while she could understand Vern's revulsion, for, on the face of it, her apparent behaviour had been reprehensible, she considered his own behaviour left him little room to criticise anyone else. His lack of trust, the fact that he hadn't even paused to wonder if there could have been extenuating circumstances, hurt, yet she couldn't bring herself to betray Jessie. And, in view of Vern's blind condemnation, she persuaded herself it couldn't matter.

The following day, however, she had known she must see Jessie to ask if she couldn't, somehow, explain at least some of the truth to her brother. Somehow, despite what Vern had done to her, Eden couldn't bear to think of him leaving Jamaica believing such terrible things of her. If Vern chose to have affairs with several women at the same time—well, that was his business, but it made Eden ill to know that he thought her capable of the same duplicity. Surely with his experience he must have been able to tell she disliked Diego Dexter intensely?

It seemed incredible that disaster could strike twice, and so quickly! Halfway to the plantation, to which she had walked, she had come across Jessie's car, crashed in a rocky dip off the road with Jessie trapped inside it. She was in the passenger seat, apparently unhurt, but there was no sign of any driver.

'Eden!' Jessie had lifted fear-filled eyes to Eden's horrified face, 'Would you go and get help—and say you were driving?'

Eden had been startled and reluctant, until Jessie had explained that Vern had sacked Diego and they had been running away together.

'I'm not hurt,' she had maintained. 'My legs are caught, but there's not even a twinge of pain. But if Vern got to know we were eloping and Diego driving, he'd throw him off the island.' With a sob she had appealed to Eden despairingly, 'We're in love, Eden!'

It hadn't been until much later that Eden had wondered how any man, no matter what the circumstances, could have left the girl he loved, as Diego had done. That didn't occur to her shocked mind immediately, though. Anxious to calm Jessie's growing hysteria, she hastily agreed to do as the other girl asked, without really considering what she was letting herself in for. Before she had had time to do more than acquiesce, one of the plantation trucks had come by and gone for help. Vern had arrived quickly, but had been too busy supervising the freeing of Jessie to spare more than a word for Eden.

To Eden's horror, Jessie had been far more severely injured than was at first apparent, and Vern had held Eden fully responsible. Jessie received medical treatment in Kingston, then Vern had taken her to the States, but before he left he had called at the house on the beach.

He had told Eden grimly that he wanted to speak to her. She had been sitting at the very spot where she was now when he found her, and she doubted if she would ever forget what he had said to her. She had felt flayed alive by the livid fury of his tongue. If she had been any other person, he had said, as she had stared blindly out to sea, he would have had her prosecuted for dangerous driving. Jessie might never recover, and it was her fault.

Eden had been dully silent throughout, having no idea how to extricate herself from the situation without putting Jessie in a position that might deprive her of her brother's much-needed help. If Vern knew the truth, mightn't she suffer even more than she was doing now? It was apparent to Eden that she had, if inadvertently, become too involved with Jessie and Diego, and

without their assistance, which was obviously not
forthcoming, there was no way she could clear herself in
Vern's eyes. It was unlikely, whatever she said, that he
would believe her. It had actually been Jessie who had
cried shrilly, as he had approached the scene of the
accident, that Eden had been driving, leaving Eden
shattered to realise that she had no means of proving
she hadn't been.

No, Vern would never credit that she had had
nothing to do with it. And she couldn't forget he had a
fiancée, which prevented her from even thinking of
trying to convince him. All these weeks he had been
deceiving her. It was true he had never said he loved
her, but he hadn't seemed reluctant to give her this
impression. It didn't seem to matter if he believed she
was a slut and had practically murdered his sister. What
difference could it make now what he thought of her?

He had been turning away, his face still pale with
anger, when something deeply hurt inside her had
driven a tortured cry from her white lips. 'Vern, do you
really hate me so much?'

This had appeared to snap something in his head.
Furiously he had grabbed hold of her, shaking her, his
hands nearly breaking her in two. Then he had kissed
her, the force of his mouth working such havoc that she
had been unable to speak afterwards.

Eden shuddered on the sands, pain shadowing the
loveliness of her thickly lashed eyes as the trauma of
remembering took a heavy toll on her slender body. As
she watched the sky slowly lightening on the horizon,
heralding the early dawn, she wondered wearily what
was going to happen next. Vern was back, and although
they had managed to keep track of Jessie's progress,
neither she nor Joe had heard anything about Vern
being married. Of Diego Dexter there had been no
proper news either. He had simply disappeared. A new
manager, George Willis, had come to take his place,

and, as far as Eden had been able to tell, things had gone on much as before.

There followed two days of what to Eden was uneasy silence before she heard from Vern again, two days during which both sleep and peace of mind curiously eluded her. Then, just as she was beginning to hope that Vern had decided to forget her, he sent a car to collect her, so she could visit his sister.

Joe raised his brows and, showing rare authority, ordered the man who had brought the message to wait outside.

As the car door slammed, he turned back to Eden. 'Are you sure you want to go?'

He was trying to tell her she didn't have to, and her heart warmed towards him. She had never told him the truth about Jessie's accident. Vern had hurt her so much she hadn't been able to trust anyone, and she had felt that to confide in Joe might only upset and worry him, especially when there had been nothing he could do. Vern had hushed everything up so that little had come to Joe's ears, but she had known he had sensed her unhappiness during the weeks after Vern had gone. It was obvious to Eden that he was thinking of this now and doing his best to protect her.

'I'll be all right, Joe,' she smiled to reassure him, even as her hands clenched tightly. 'I'd like to see Jessie.'

She could have refused to go. As Joe indirectly pointed out, no one could make her, and she felt a twinge of guilt for pretending she was going entirely because of Vern's sister. She was sorry for Jessie, but the other girl had used her shamelessly and she didn't feel she owed her anything. It was Vern who Eden was aware she had to see again. The evening at the club had taken on all the dimensions of a bad dream. She found it impossible to believe she still cared for him as much as ever and she was sure that as soon as she met him again she would realise she had made a mistake.

Surprise and shock had probably distorted her ability to feel or even think clearly before.

On the way to the plantation, Eden closed her eyes as the car drove past the spot where Jessie had been injured and didn't open them again until the car drew up outside Vern's door. Nothing appeared to have changed. The house seemed exactly the same as the last time she had seen it—still large and rambling with an air of neglect. Yet it appealed to her, as it had always done, and she knew if ever she had had the chance, she could have lived here happily.

If the house hadn't changed, Vern had. She was so absorbed in her surroundings that she didn't, at first, notice him coming down the wide stone steps to meet her. At the sound of his footsteps she glanced round with surprise and saw immediately that her former impressions hadn't been completely wrong.

He was still big and tough-looking, but the lines of his face were more deeply carved than she recalled. His hair was as dark as ever, but there were streaks of grey at his temples and a cold bleakness in his eyes which she didn't remember, except, perhaps on the last occasion she had seen him, two years ago.

As she stumbled on the gravel at his feet, she could almost feel the deep antagonism between them. It clawed and clutched at her, tightening her nerves like the grasp of a giant hand until she could scarcely breathe. It was something she had never experienced before, it was as if a dagger was twisting inside her, and she thought yearningly of the warm, gentle feelings of other days. Vern had always been able to excite her, but she couldn't remember anything like the fierceness of the emotions consuming her now.

When he grasped her arm, far from gently, drawing her quickly into the house, she tried to stay cool. She hadn't expected to see him as soon and she felt again the old, unsteady beat of her heart. On the way here, it had suddenly occurred to her that he might not be at home, and she wasn't sure whether to be glad or sorry that he was. She only wished that he had allowed her more time to get a proper grip on herself before he had put in an appearance.

'Come and meet everyone,' he broke the silence as though there had been no silence at all. He spoke smoothly, both his voice and face quite without expression.

'You have guests?'

'Don't look so put out.' He still spoke smoothly but as Eden glanced at him in dismay, she noticed he was studying her and shrank from the studied insolence in his eyes. 'A few guests won't hurt you.'

He made it sound as though nothing could, and her face paled. 'You could have told me!'

'What difference could it have made?'

Eden might have said she would have dressed differently. It made her bitter to realise, as she glanced briefly at the shabby cotton skirt she was wearing, that she hadn't anything better to put on. If she had known there were other people here, apart from Jessie, she could have refused to come, though. As Joe had hinted, no one could have made her!

When she didn't reply, Vern tightened his grip on her arm, deliberately thrusting her before him. 'We'd better go in,' he said curtly.

Several people had gathered in the drawing-room. She remembered the last time Vern had asked her here, when they had had tea together, and silently berated herself for her obsession with the past. The past was dead, nothing could change that!

Jessie was sitting down, but as Eden entered the room with Vern she came quickly towards them. Noting her clumsy movements, Eden wondered why she bothered, then suddenly, instinctively, she knew. Walking with a limp, one of Jessie's legs seemed slightly shorter than the other and shapeless around the ankle. Jessie, Eden realised, was appealing for her sympathy. She was showing Eden quite clearly how crippled she was so that Eden, if she had been tempted, wouldn't denounce her.

Eden was stunned, however, when she held out her hand and Jessie ignored it. She stifled a gasp as she understood the full deviousness of Jessie's motives. She was making it quite plain that she couldn't yet bring herself to touch the girl who had been responsible for the accident which had so injured her.

'Surely you can't be surprised?' she heard Vern murmur harshly in her ear. 'You stole her man and maimed her for life. What did you expect?'

Eden felt herself going as cold as ice as he gently guided Jessie to her chair again before introducing Eden to the others. There wasn't the crowd which Eden's dazed eyes had appeared to see when she first caught sight of them. In actual fact, there was only an aunt of Vern's, a Mrs Frobisher, come from the States to help Jessie, and two people from Kingston. The latter, Vern introduced as Martin Darel and Carita, his sister.

Why had Vern thought it necessary to invite her here today as well? Eden wondered hollowly. Mrs Frobisher and Martin Darel were pleasant and seemed pleased to meet her, but Miss Darel looked as though she would have liked to have followed Jessie's lead and ignored her. Was this the girl whom Vern had taken to the races in Kingston, when he was supposed to have been there on business? Her name seemed oddly familiar. She wouldn't be much younger than he was and she was beautiful, with the kind of sophistication he was used to and obviously appreciated. Eden squirmed as she tried not to guess what he must have thought of her own adolescent gaucheness.

After smiling seductively at him, Carita went back to rejoin Jessie at the other side of the room, but before she went she took time to allow her eyes to slide contemptuously over Eden's shabby skirt, leaving Eden in no doubt as to her exact opinion of it!

Wishing more fervently by the minute that she had never come, Eden smiled gratefully as Mrs Frobisher poured her a cup of tea and told her to find herself a seat. She chose one near a heavily curtained alcove. She didn't think Mrs Frobisher had meant her to go as far away, but it was suddenly imperative to put as much distance between herself and Vern as possible. Jessie obviously didn't want her. As soon as she could, without arousing speculation, she would go home. Everything here disturbed her much more than she had ever imagined it would, and she couldn't stop herself from trembling.

Vern came and sat beside her, and, as his leg touched hers, she wished belatedly that she had chosen a chair rather than a settee. Unable not to be conscious of the coldly curious glances Carita was darting at her, she thought the other girl wouldn't have looked so annoyed if she could have seen the hate in Vern's eyes and heard what he was saying to her.

'You see how Jessie is?'

Eden put her cup down unsteadily on the table in front of her, then pushed her hands underneath her for fear he should notice how they were shaking. 'She has a bad limp.'

He never took his eyes off her and his voice was hard with anger. 'So you concede that much?'

She stared at her tea, as if it was some new and terribly interesting beverage. 'At least she must be able to get around.'

'She does, but she still suffers.'

'Don't we all!'

'Eden!' he exclaimed, low-toned but sharp. 'I find it impossible to believe you can be so insensitive, although if you hadn't been you would never have taken Dexter from Jessie in the first place and then had the nerve to ask to drive her car.'

That Jessie had obviously told him nothing didn't hurt half as much as Vern's almost tangible dislike and distrust. Yet what could she do? Eden squirmed like a worm on a pin, unable to help herself. 'You never thought much of Diego,' she retorted impulsively, but speaking the truth, 'If it hadn't been for what happened he might have been your brother-in-law.'

'That's not the point, though, is it?' he came back furiously. 'How many lovers have you had since then, Eden?'

Her voice a thin whisper of pain, she replied, 'You wouldn't believe I wasn't lying if I said none.'

'I'm no fool.' He stared at her exquisite profile, sweat breaking out on his brow.

Eden saw it as she swung her head to gaze at him, her huge eyes mutely appealing, although she didn't know it. He must care for Jessie a lot, but of course a man like him would naturally care for his family. Mrs Frobisher clearly adored him, and blood ties always counted for a lot. 'I think I'd like to leave,' she told him. 'You can't possibly want someone like me here.'

'Oh, no, you don't!' His hand shot out to almost haul her back to his side when she would have jumped to her feet. 'You're finished with cheating, my child. You're going to stay and help Jessie to renew her interest in life, which indirectly means her faith in people. And I mean to be around to see that you do it!'

Could there be worse fates? Eden trembled as she fell half on top of him and struggled to escape his brutal hands, while from across the width of the drawing-room they were regarded with varying degrees of interest.

Vern must have realised they were being watched, but that didn't appear to bother him. He let Eden edge a few inches away from him, but he kept hold of her arm, which, by the grip of his fingers, she knew would be bruised in the morning. Drawing a deep breath, she tried to control her leaping senses. The prospect of bruising didn't bother her nearly as much as the sensations she was experiencing from the grasp he had on her.

'What about your girl-friend over there?' she muttered desperately. 'Don't you realise that this kind of thing——' she flicked a speaking glance at his restraining hand, 'is making her wonder?'

'You've still got an outsize imagination,' he returned derisively. 'Once you imagined I was in love with you. It amused me at the time, but not any more.'

Eden couldn't see the connection. What could Carita Darel have to do with what had happened between Vern and herself? And Vern didn't need to tell her he had merely been amusing himself. If he had loved her at all he couldn't have condemned her so easily.

'I realise you never cared for me seriously.' There was flat acceptance in her voice. She thought of the girl in the States whom Jessie had said he was in love with. Almost choking, she added, 'I—we heard you might be married.'

'I'm not.' He spoke so forcibly she had to believe him, but any relief she might have felt was swept aside by the icy coldness of his eyes. 'Look at me, Eden.'

'What is it?' she gasped, trying to fight and deny the sharp shaft of something which instantly seared them together. 'Dear heaven!' she whispered, suddenly trembling.

Vern laughed harshly. 'So you still feel it? There may be no love, but whatever there is is taking an unconscionable time in dying. There might be only one way of purging it completely from our systems!'

'You must be crazy,' she said hoarsely, not fully understanding and not sure that she wanted to.

He eyed her grimly. 'Would one more lover more or

less make any difference? Especially one who wouldn't disappoint you.'

'Have you ever thought,' she was stunned to hear herself shoot back, 'that if I found one who didn't I might want to hang on to him?'

He looked as though he would have liked to hit her as his eyes smouldered on her white face. 'Don't worry,' he snarled, 'I was merely speculating, not immediately applying for the position.'

Eden felt herself visibly quiver and a quick rush of pink stained her cheeks. She had to look away to stop herself from watching his long, lithe body. In his fawn slacks and thin shirt, which emphasised his deep chest and broad shoulders, despite her embarrassment over what she had just said, he had a dangerous attraction which her starved senses were much too aware of. Even his thick dark hair brought back memories of how her fingers had tingled when they had threaded their way through it. Did one never forget? she wondered, gazing at him wearily.

'You hate me, don't you?' she sighed, thinking what a waste of time loving him had been.

CHAPTER FIVE

'HATE isn't quite the right word.'

As the green eyes glinted coldly, Eden drew back from the hard stare. Vern certainly knew how to hurt and wound, every word he uttered might have been a dagger. She couldn't remember him ever being like this with her before. Perhaps if he hadn't been as gentle with her two years ago, she wouldn't have noticed such a difference now.

Before she could think of a reply not so impulsive as one of her previous ones, Martin Darel approached, clearly not intimidated by Vern's unwelcoming stare, which might have stopped another man in his tracks.

Unperturbed, Martin glanced at Eden as he spoke to him. 'You can't expect to keep such a beautiful young lady all to yourself.' Smiling, he asked, 'Do you mind if I join you?'

He was younger than his sister and had a determined gleam in his eye which Eden hadn't noticed when she'd shaken hands with him. She wasn't sure that she liked it, but nevertheless, when he turned to her she shook her head and smiled back. He had saved her when she had been ready to burst into tears because of Vern's taunting remarks and she was grateful.

Vern wasn't similarly appeased. He was annoyed by the interruption, she could tell, but, Martin being a guest, there was nothing he could do about it. Yet the silent vibrations coming from him only amused her fleetingly. They were too threatening to do anything but arouse eventual apprehension.

With a shudder she wrenched her attention back to

Martin Darel, nervously keeping it there. 'I don't mind, but I was just about to go and speak to Jessie.'

Abruptly Vern stood up, dragging Eden with him. 'Make yourself comfortable, Martin.' Mockingly his head inclined towards the seat he had just vacated.

Martin didn't take the hint. He would have a hide like a rhinoceros when it suited him! Eden lowered her heavy lashes as he followed them to where Jessie and his sister were sitting, for some reason wanting to keep her opinion of him to herself. By her side, Vern's face was without expression, but she sensed that underneath he was seething.

At the end of a difficult hour, Eden judged she might reasonably ask to go home. Vern ordered the car for her and saw her out. Jessie had scarcely spoken to her. Eden guessed she had decided to adopt an ostrich-like attitude and meant to keep her head down in the hope that Eden wouldn't come again. If her brother had thought she needed Eden's company, Jessie, quite clearly, was not of the same opinion.

'Lay off Martin!' Vern snapped savagely, as they crossed the hall.

Eden almost fled through the front door. 'I don't have to listen to your horrible insinuations!' she retorted angrily. 'I'd probably only be wasting my time if I said I didn't know what you were talking about!'

'Don't you?' His mouth curled nastily as his hand shot out to halt her ruthlessly, out of earshot of the curious driver. 'Do you think I wasn't aware of all the palpitating little signals you were throwing out—in his direction!'

'You're crazy . . .'

He broke in. 'I find your constant repetition of that remark boring. I brought Darel here for Jessie's sake, not yours. She might take an interest in him, so, as I said, lay off!'

For sheer insolence he must take some beating! Eden

glared at him, too upset to be discreet. 'It has to be mutual, you know! You can't just wrap a man up and present him to a woman like a gift. Not, say, like a—a pair of earrings!'

She wasn't sure why she had mentioned the earrings so fiercely, and in a way which clearly revealed that she had meant the pair he had given her and that she had thought nothing of them. It didn't make sense when she loved them so much. Perhaps it was her tired mind hitting out blindly, fixing on a highly improbable way of hurting him as he was hurting her.

'What did you do with my earrings?' He made no attempt to hide the fresh rage in his eyes, or to pretend he didn't know which ones she was talking about.

A faint colour stole to Eden's pale cheeks. Before he had gone to the States she had rarely taken them off. Now she slept with them under her pillow and looked at them frequently during the day.

'I sold them,' she lied.

'You—what!'

'You heard.'

'Why, you little thief! They belonged to my family!' Clearly regretting the presence of a third party, Vern obviously exerted a strong control over himself as he almost threw Eden into the waiting car. The fury transmitted through the grip of his steely fingers, was painful but something she was getting used to. 'I'll see you in a day or two,' he snapped, 'when I feel less like strangling you!'

During the next few days Eden worried constantly over the earrings. Vern would naturally be upset as they had belonged to his grandmother. She deeply regretted saying she had parted with them. If she had intended making him angry she had certainly succeeded, but she couldn't help feeling bad about it.

Then Joe was being secretive again. He had gone to Kingston, declaring he had some business to attend to, and hadn't allowed Eden to go with him. Why he should specially want to go to Kingston had puzzled Eden but not bothered her over much. It was his quietness since he had returned which made her suspect he was hiding something from her.

After supper one evening, she went for a long walk. Joe's continuing silence was beginning to bother her more than a little, and this, combined with her deep unhappiness over Vern, made her feel she had to get out of the house. On top of this, Fay Derwent had called, ostensibly to see how Eden was after her slight malaise at the club dance, but taking the opportunity to tell her that as the height of the tourist season was over, she had decided to indulge in a holiday, so was running her stocks down.

Eden didn't begrudge Fay a holiday. She could never remember her taking one before, so she must deserve one. What worried Eden was that she might have no money coming in until Fay returned. And, as she hinted that she had almost decided to marry Robert and go with him to Europe, heaven knew when that might be. Fay, though not being absolutely certain of Eden's circumstances, had offered to lend her something to tide her over, but Eden's pride had forced her to refuse.

Absorbed by anxious thoughts, Eden didn't get back to the house until the light was fading. To her despair she found Vern there, talking to her father.

She hadn't seen him since that dreadful afternoon when they had quarrelled. She hadn't seen Jessie, either, or the Darels. As far as Jessie was concerned, Eden thought she could read her like a book. As Jessie hadn't told Vern the truth about her accident or Diego Dexter, she would see no point in mentioning anything now. She would probably be unwilling to confess even minor details, no matter what anyone said to her, as she couldn't, or believed she couldn't, do without his support and protection. In fairness to Jessie, Eden knew she hadn't known of the deepening friendship between herself and Vern, but sometimes she wondred if it would have made any difference. Jessie, being naturally selfish, might always consider her own interests first.

Eden almost turned and ran when she first saw Vern. If it hadn't been for her stubborn pride, she might have done. She could tell from his narrowed glance as he swung round, catching her hesitating by the living-room door, that he expected her to.

'Don't run away, Eden,' he said curtly.

Because Joe was there, she walked forward slowly. She didn't have to feel so shaken and nervous, she told herself. At the worst, Vern could only be here to ask her to visit Jessie again.

Joe turned to glance at her, running his fingers through his sparse hair. 'You might make some coffee, Eden, now you're back. We're thirsty.'

Eden was surprised. At this time of night Joe usually drank beer or whisky, but as Vern didn't refuse or say anything about being in a hurry, she felt obliged to do as he asked. The mundane task of boiling water and grinding fresh coffee did, however, give her a chance to pull herself together.

On returning to the living-room a little later, with a laden tray, she tried not to look at where Vern was sitting. As she appeared again, he rose to help her and she wished he hadn't. When his fingers brushed hers, as he relieved her of the tray, she almost jumped. Surely, she prayed, he won't be long in going?

'Thank you,' she murmured stiffly, feeling anything but grateful.

She didn't notice what Joe was doing until she saw him shuffling uneasily in his chair. Usually he slumped, like a dead weight, paying little attention to anything or anyone, if he wasn't reading. A terrible suspicion suddenly shook her. Something seemed to have upset him. Could Vern possibly have been telling him the truth—or what he thought was the truth, about Jessie's accident?

'Is anything wrong, Dad?' She used the name he disliked, without thinking, she was so apprehensive.

He glanced up quickly, as she came over to gaze down on him. 'Not exactly,' he muttered cautiously.

Vern interrupted sardonically. 'It might be more accurate to say that your father finds he's faced with a bit of a dilemma.'

Joe had been away, alone, mysteriously. Eden went cold as she wondered what mischief he had got up to. He had never been a gambling man, although he liked what he called a flutter. She suspected, if he had been able to afford it, he would have gone to the casino or racecourse more often. Was that what he had been doing in Kingston? Had he been to Caymanas racetrack and got in debt?

'Were you at the races on Wednesday?' she demanded, ignoring Vern.

'I was, but it's not that,' he replied. Still clearly uneasy, he glanced past her to Vern. 'You'd better tell her.'

By this time Eden's nerves were so bad she could have shouted at them both. Vern had taken it upon himself to pour three cups of coffee, his narrowed glance flicking occasionally from Eden to Joe. The watchful cast of his face was hard to read. He's ruthless, she thought, his charm is only skin deep. He uses it to get his own way, as, she felt instinctively, he was bent on doing now.

'What your father finds so difficult to explain, Eden,' he said curtly, 'is that he's been made an offer for the house and the land he owns by a hotel company.'

'What!'

Joe looked at her anxiously.

Eden's eyes widened incredulously, her young face strained and aghast. 'You haven't agreed?' she whispered hoarsely, too stunned, right then, to consider the advantages. All she could think of was bulldozers and tons of bricks and concrete. Oh, they would build something stupendous, architecturally acceptable, she had no doubt, but before that happened they would have destroyed a lot of natural beauty, which no builder, however clever, could replace.

When Joe didn't reply, she flung herself on her knees beside his chair. 'Dad, don't!' she begged. 'It—it would be like sacrilege!'

'And it would kill me,' Joe sighed.

'Then what's the problem?' Eden frowned as Vern stirred, as though deliberately reminding them of his presence. Angrily she turned her head to look at him. 'Where do you come in? Or are you merely offering neighbourly advice?'

'If you care to put it that way,' he replied coolly, 'yes.'

'You're kidding!' Eden knew that must sound childish, but she had discovered, in times of stress, that words from her adolescent vocabulary often served best.

Joe cut in, somewhat wearily, 'It's more than that, Eden. We're desperately short of money, I'll have to do something, but my grandfather stipulated in his will that if ever I should decide to sell the property, the Lomaxes were to have first refusal.'

Eden trembled as her shocked glance jerked back to Vern. 'Do you want it?'

'Certainly.'

'Why have you never mentioned this before?' Eden asked Joe raggedly.

'I would have done—eventually,' he replied.

Vern said, clearly anticipating Eden's next query, 'Your father's grandfather and mine were great friends, Eden, and were both keen conservationists. Neither of them wanted to see the flora and fauna of this part of the coast destroyed, which must be why your great-grandfather made this condition in his will. The Lomaxes were a wealthy and powerful family then—perhaps he thought it was one way of making sure we were given the chance to look after it.'

This made sense, but only in so far as it went. Something told Eden that the next few minutes could be crucial. 'I see,' she tried to speak coolly. 'What I don't understand is why that should have any particular relevance at the moment. Surely,' she begged Joe urgently, 'you don't have to sell if you don't want to? We'll manage somehow—And that's not something Vern need concern himself with.'

Joe eyed his daughter unhappily, as if the sight of her vulnerable young face pained him. 'I'm tired of struggling, Eden. It never came naturally to me, even when I was younger, and lately, whenever I've thought of the future, I've been extremely depressed. When a man called a few days ago and suggested I might like to sell out, it seemed a good idea.'

'Where was I?'

'Swimming on the reef, honey. I arranged to meet one of his chief executives in Kingston. As you didn't see him, I didn't think there was much point in mentioning it until I returned.'

'You haven't agreed to anything yet?' she implored. 'You haven't signed anything?'

'No. I was tempted, but I had to see Vern first.'

'But why?' she cried, appealing to him despairingly. 'You've just said that to leave here would kill you.'

'Listen, darling.' With an air of hopelessness, Joe came to his feet, ignoring the coffee he had asked for. 'It all depends on you, but I don't think I can explain. I'll have to leave it to Vern—he will. I'll go to bed and see you in the morning. Or you can look in and tell me of your decision later. If you come to one, that is.'

As Eden stared in speechless bewilderment after his

retreating figure, she heard Vern saying quietly, 'You'd better sit down, Eden.'

'I can't.' She was suddenly so shaken by some oppressive dread pressing down on her that she found it impossible to do anything but stare at him apprehensively. 'What is it that Dad finds impossible to tell me? He's never been like this before. Has he promised to sell to you without asking me first? Is that it?'

Stepping nearer, Vern took hold of her arm. 'Let's go outside and walk,' he suggested curtly. 'You might find it easier outside to hear what I have to say.'

It had grown dark but, as usual, the stars were so bright they needed no other light. A small animal or sea creature scuttled out of their way as they went along the shore and a piece of shell crunched under Vern's foot. Eden became slowly aware that she had obeyed him without thinking and was stumbling blindly by his side.

'Please!' she whispered, unable to bear the suspense any longer.

Vern's mouth twisted as her agitation relayed clearly through the darkness. 'I'm going to buy the house and land, Eden,' he told her abruptly. 'Joe wants to sell it to me, and you shouldn't be angry with him. He's only thinking of your future.'

'My future?' she exclaimed hoarsely. 'But neither of us is old yet! If we had been I could have understood.'

'Your father isn't getting any younger,' Vern said dryly. 'The hotel company offered him a lot of money and he knows they're going to keep on at him until he gives in. He also knows that whatever he gets, he stands a good chance of losing it.'

'How?'

'I'll put it this way,' Vern replied with cold patience. 'No hotel company would allow him to live here. If he sold to them he would have to leave, and he would be unhappy. Then the rot would set in, call it by any name

you like—gambling, drink, women. Within a short time
he would have nothing left. I'd stake my life on it.'

Eden stumbled on the sand. The sea was a soothing
sound as it lapped the damp shingle at their feet, but for
once she was deaf to its soporific appeal. The feeling of
dread hadn't lifted, if anything it was getting worse.

'And what can you offer instead?' she asked stonily,
trying to ignore the warmth of his big body pressed
against her side as he tightened his grip on her arm.
'You would presumably do much the same thing. I
mean, you'd pay us a lot of money and put us out of
our home.'

'Your father could stay. I've already told him that.'

'What about me?'

'You would become my wife, so that Joe would know
you would always be looked after.'

Eden felt the stars spinning round her. 'Is this your
idea of a joke?' she cried.

'No,' he assured her grimly, slipping his arm
completely around her, as if he guessed she was in need
of extra support. 'I need a wife and Joe wants an
income for life, so we made a bargain.'

'Just like that!' Eden couldn't believe Joe would do
this to her. She wanted to run back to the house and
beg him to tell her it wasn't true!

'It wasn't just like that.' Vern brought her faltering
footsteps to a halt and stared tersely down on her.
'Joe's anxious about you. He realises if anything
happened to him you'd be quite alone in the world.
You could go to your mother, but who knows what
might happen to you before you got there.'

'I wouldn't go to her.'

'Well then, why not be sensible and do as he asks?'

'Wait a minute!' Eden gulped, wishing she could
think straight. 'How much money would you be paying
Dad?'

'So much a week,' Vern retorted curtly. 'It would be

safer for him that way. We would naturally have a
proper agreement drawn up, but I couldn't afford to
give him a lump sum.'

Eden shook her head, still puzzled. 'I can't see why I
should come into it at all.'

'Because, as I've just told you, I need a wife, and the
kind of woman I would like to marry would never take
on a penniless planter.'

'Penniless?' Eden gasped angrily. 'Why, you must be
wealthy!'

'My family was, once,' he admitted grimly, 'but my
father lost a great deal of money. When he died I
discovered we were deeply in debt. If it hadn't been for
the part of the business in the States which I was
running, we might have lost everything. That's what
I've been doing these past two years, expanding that in
order to pay off what was owed. When that was done
and Jessie out of hospital, I knew I had to make a
choice between the States and Jamaica, and the
plantation won. Unfortunately that means I'm having
to learn to live very frugally, with all the restrictions
which reduced circumstances normally impose.'

So that must be why he hadn't married Miss Darel,
or the girl in the States. Instead of the well-bred girl he
would like, he was having to settle for what he could
get! Bitterly, Eden stared at him. 'Until you can afford
the kind of wife you obviously believe you deserve, why
not take a mistress?'

She saw the glint of his teeth in the starlight but
somehow didn't think he was amused. 'A mistress can
be time-consuming and expensive, two things I can't
afford.'

'Why marry at all?' Eden whispered with hot cheeks,
suspecting he was paying her out for mentioning a
mistress in the first place.

She sensed he was still annoyed as he retorted, 'As
I've just told you, I won't have time to go traipsing all

over the place, looking for entertainment. I need a wife, because I want sons before I'm very much older. I want someone who will help with Jessie as well, and not many women might be willing to do that. But you won't be able to refuse,' he said harshly, 'as you're the one responsible for her being as she is.'

Eden hadn't thought her cheeks could grow so hot or her heart as cold. What kind of a proposal was that, with every sentence being almost an insult! He couldn't expect her to agree. No girl with any sense in her head would!

'I'll talk to Dad,' she said unevenly. 'I'll have to persuade him we can go on as we are.'

'He won't listen.'

'Then I'll advise him to settle for the hotel company. I'm afraid you'll have to look elsewhere for a wife.'

Vern's mouth twisted cynically at her angry tones. 'According to the will, he's not allowed to refuse any reasonable offer from me.'

'And you call your offer reasonable?' she choked.

'You'd have some difficulty in finding a lawyer to say it wasn't,' he snapped, 'and I'm very familiar with the law, Eden.'

'But you despise me!'

'That's of little consequence, weighed against everything else.'

She looked down, wishing that for once she could puncture his cool self-confidence, see some of the assurance wiped from his autocratic face. It took a lot of effort to restrain herself from shouting at him and remain calm. She might be wiser to try and be as clever as he was. Wasn't there such a thing as auto-suggestion?

'Isn't there anyone in the States who loves you and wouldn't mind being poor?' she asked, 'whom you'd rather be married to?'

He laughed shortly. 'It wouldn't be possible, anyway. And I want this land.'

'But . . .'

'Let's not speculate any longer, Eden,' he crushed any further appeal before she had a chance to voice it. 'All you have to do is say yes, we can go on from there. If it helps, I hinted to Joe that we'd been falling in love two years ago, before I went away, but my financial status and Jessie's accident forced me to call a halt. It shouldn't be hard to convince him that we've made up our differences, especially in the light of what has just arisen.'

Eden suddenly realised she was still standing practically in Vern's arms, and with a furious gasp she jerked herself away from him. 'You have a nerve!'

'Be careful,' he warned. 'You don't want me losing my temper as well. I'm trying to be reasonable.'

'You seem,' she retorted hotly, 'to imply that I've no choice but to accept your—repulsive offer!'

'I don't believe you have much room for manoeuvre,' he agreed tightly, 'and neither will you, when you calm down enough to think sensibly about it.'

She stared at him, conscious of feeling trapped and sick. 'How long do I have?'

He turned to walk the few yards back to the house, leaving her with no option but to follow. He didn't ask to come in again and she was just about to repeat her question when he answered coldly, 'I'll give you until the day after tomorrow. That should be long enough for anyone. But,' he warned sharply, 'be sure and think carefully, because I shan't give you a second chance.'

She didn't suppose he would, Eden thought dully, gazing after him with frightened eyes as he disappeared in the darkness towards his car.

Eden hadn't thought it possible to argue so long and sensibly with oneself and still come to the same crazy conclusion. She spent all night mulling over Vern's incredible proposal without finding a solution to Joe's problem which would involve only him.

She was ready to admit that much of what Vern had said could be true. If Joe was to sell to a property developer for a large lump sum, it could prove disastrous. Joe had never considered money important, which must be why it always slipped through his fingers like water and, somehow, she couldn't contemplate the probability, if she turned Vern down, of seeing him finish up as Vern said he might. She suspected it was only because he was worried about the future that he had thought of money now.

And if, as Vern stated, they couldn't refuse his offer, what then? There might be such a thing as having too much money, but how did one manage without any? It could be months before she found a job or, as Fay was going away, someone else willing to buy her paintings. Could she possibly stand by and risk seeing Joe starve?

Dawn found Eden hollow-eyed and miserable because of the growing certainty at the back of her mind, which she wasn't quite ready to face, of what she must do. She hadn't gone to Joe's room the night before, although she was aware he might have been expecting—even hoping—to see her. Before she spoke to him again she had suddenly realised she must come to a definite decision.

Vern wanted this land because he had no wish to see his plantation overrun by tourists. While she could sympathise with him over this, she couldn't admire him for the lengths he was obviously prepared to go to to prevent that happening. In telling Joe that he and his daughter had been falling in love, he had limited the strength of any attack she might have made on his ridiculous suggestions. If she was to deny that they had been growing fond of each other, he would know as well as she did that Joe might never allow her to marry him.

If she were to deny she had ever cared for Vern, besides being a lie, it would be impossible to change her mind later. Joe wouldn't believe her if she did, and hadn't Vern said he wouldn't give her another chance? He might only be bluffing, of course, but how could she know for sure?

Feeling feverish, Eden crawled from her bed and put on her bikini, fatalistically aware there was only one course open to her. She had to marry Vern, even knowing how much he despised her, and all the unhappiness that would bring. But before telling Joe this, she must have a swim. It seemed to Eden that she had to have a few more minutes to herself in order to strengthen her wavering resolution and convince herself she was doing the right thing.

The following morning, when Vern called, she told him she would marry him, and he immediately began making plans for their wedding. She had managed to hide her fear and unhappiness from Joe, who was clearly delighted with her decision and told her, with such frequency that she tried not to scream, of his former doubts. When he kept smiling to himself and remarking how kind fate was and how thankful he was at the way things had turned out, Eden found it difficult to stop herself from rounding on him hysterically and telling him to speak for himself.

She suspected Vern had known all along that she was caught like a mouse in a trap and had given her a day longer than was necessary. He didn't say anything, but she could see from the sheer confidence of his expression, when he arrived, that he didn't expect to be turned down. His face might have gone a little pale when she had told him she was willing to marry him, but she assumed this was because he had had fleeting doubts over parting with his own freedom.

He didn't want to wait, he said firmly. Two days might have been enough, but they had better settle for two weeks as he wanted an agreement for Joe drawn up and Eden would want to have some time to shop for her trousseau.

'I won't want much,' she said quickly, then felt mortified as she realised this might make him believe she would rather have married him in a hurry.

'I want my bride properly dressed,' he said curtly, on returning in the evening after Joe had gone to bed, to find her alone. 'I didn't want to argue with you in front of Joe, this morning, but we'll go to Montego Bay tomorrow.'

She had to say it. Rubbing the palms of her suddenly perspiring hands down the sides of her ragged shorts, she took a deep breath. 'I can't afford it, Vern, neither can Joe. And it's not as if I'm going to be a proper bride.'

'Come again?' His eyes narrowed darkly.

'Don't!' she quivered, her nerves tightening painfully against such deliberate obtuseness. 'Ours won't be a normal marriage, will it? I won't need a lot of clothes.'

Ignoring, for the moment, her reference to clothes, he said coolly, 'I thought I mentioned sons?'

She flushed, her heart beginning to beat furiously, and, knowing Vern was responsible, hating him for it. 'I didn't think you were serious. After all . . .'

As her voice trailed off in embarrassment, his mouth curled. 'Surely you aren't trying to tell me that you don't believe people can have a family unless they're in love? Perhaps that's how you imagine you've escaped so far?'

The implications of what he said were so obvious that she felt like weeping. He was stating plainly that he didn't love her and that he believed she had had numerous affairs with other men.

'I'd rather you treated me like another employee,' she whispered, turning away from him so he wouldn't see her hurt.

'Oh, I'll do that,' he bit out, 'but I want someone in my bed as well. It will help to keep up appearances, and men in these parts are men, as you've no doubt already discovered.'

As though to emphasise his point, he caught her arms, swinging her round and back to him as he lowered his head. It was the first time he had kissed her since the night of the club dance, and she shivered as his mouth touched her lips briefly before forcing them apart. Then he drew her closer, one hand settling over her hips while the other found its way under her brief top, sending flickers of fire down her spine. As her strength disappeared, his fingers slid round to caress the rounded curves of her breasts and the kiss deepened as her breath caught. She tried to draw away, terrified by the force of what she recognised as merely the beginnings of her own response, but she was unprepared for the harshness with which he thrust her from him.

He pushed his hands in his pockets, his eyes glittering. 'Don't imagine by pretending to be frigid you can hope to escape me. I'm not paying for something and keeping it on ice.'

Distressed, she shook her head, pulling down her top. 'You've got the wrong impression of me somehow,' she stammered, her face hot. 'I don't have affairs.'

Vern's voice hardened contemptuously. 'It could be that you've never had the courage, but after finding you in the arms of a man like Diego Dexter, I find it hard to believe.'

'Vern——' she began.

'Don't let's argue over it,' he cut in curtly. 'How about some coffee?'

He picked her up early the next morning, and to Eden's surprise his aunt, Mrs Frobisher, was with him.

'I asked Faith to come along to give you a hand,' he said, as Eden came to meet him. 'I asked Jessie as well, but she's feeling tired.'

The harsh reproach in his tones smote her. Unhappily she wondered if he would ever forgive her for what he thought she had done to his sister.

'I'm sorry,' she said stiffly, trying not to be relieved that if she had to shop for clothes, she wasn't going to have to do it under Jessie's scornful gaze.

Mrs Frobisher left the car to bestow a cool kiss on Eden's cheek. Eden sensed that Vern's engagement had bewildered her, although she tried to hide it.

'Such a surprise!' she exclaimed. 'Vern forgets I'm getting too old to cope with such things. He might have dropped a hint!'

Vern overheard and muttered dryly, 'I told you, Faith, it happened very suddenly.'

Looking remarkably spruce, Joe joined them, with a sympathetic glance at Eden's pink cheeks. 'How are you, Faith? I'm delighted with the news.'

'Oh, Joe!' Mrs Frobisher grasped the hand he held out in both of hers, with what appeared to Eden to be a sigh of relief. 'Of course, I am too, but as I've just been saying to Eden, it's been such a surprise! When Vern brought her to tea the other day, I'm afraid I didn't quite catch her name, and she was gone before I realised she was your daughter, or that she and Vern were in love.'

CHAPTER SIX

MONTEGO BAY was Jamaica's second largest town. Like most other places in the West Indies, it had a fairly turbulent history, but was now a famous tourist resort with its own airport and plenty of good shops. It could be roughly divided into three areas. The coastal strip with its luxury hotels and shopping plazas, the hills behind and the urban district. As it was the so-called off season, Eden noticed that the streets weren't nearly as crowded as usual.

Mrs Frobisher, having shopped here often, knew exactly where to go. Eden was grateful that she had talked almost without ceasing since they had left home as it had covered the strained silence between Vern and herself. Mrs Frobisher seemed very excited about the wedding. Eden thought wryly that it might have been her own.

She told Vern exactly where to drop them off, then shooed him away. As he had an appointment, he went without protest, but Eden stared uncertainly after him.

'Come on, child!' Mrs Frobisher tugged her arm impatiently. 'Some women like having a man around when they're choosing clothes, but I don't. I think they get in the way.'

Eden wasn't so sure, although she turned obediently. 'Last night he said he was coming with me.'

'That was perhaps before I offered to,' Faith smiled happily, marching Eden into a modern boutique. 'I'm not saying he doesn't know a lot about women's clothes, but he can't know as much as I do. Besides, I believe a girl's trousseau should come as a surprise to the man she's marrying. It shouldn't be something he's seen beforehand.'

Or paid for! Eden thought bitterly.

'Now this shop,' Mrs Frobisher went on, as an assistant approached, 'has a lot of nice young things— bare shoulders, bare midriffs, the likes of that. I used to come here a lot with Jessie. Of course you don't have to take anything you don't like—there are plenty of other places.'

'I don't want to spend too much,' Eden whispered unhappily, as they were ushered to some chairs in the cool, tiled salon. She hoped Mrs Frobisher wasn't thinking of anything extravagant. Even if Vern had still been wealthy she wouldn't have wanted to spend his money and she had only a little of her own.

While Mrs Frobisher didn't, or pretended she didn't hear, Eden's mind slid back to when Joe had pressed a small wad of dollar bills in her bag, as they were leaving. When she had tried to protest, he had explained that it was part of a nest egg he had been saving for just such an occasion. Without attracting Vern's attention, she hadn't been able to do anything but accept what he had given her, but she still felt uneasy. Now she didn't know whether to spend Joe's money, which he probably couldn't afford, or let Vern pay for everything.

'Mrs Frobisher——' she began.

'Oh, call me Faith,' Mrs Frobisher exclaimed, 'or you could make it Aunt Faith. I like the prefix, although Vern ignores it.'

'Aunt Faith,' Eden swallowed, unable not to like this warmhearted, gutsy woman, even if she was bent on having her own way. 'Couldn't we go to a—well, another place, not quite so expensive?'

'No!' Faith smiled approvingly on the variety of beautiful clothes being paraded before them. 'I was a fashion designer before I married Vern's mother's brother, so I know that some of these things will suit you. Just leave it to me.'

Were all the Lomaxes and their relations so domineering? Eden wondered, gazing anxiously at the lovely, colourful fabrics, silk-screened on the island. She put out a hand to finger a length of gauzy material almost reverently. Such things were tempting, she had to admit.

She heard Faith saying, 'We can buy some material and I'll make you some dresses for when you return from your honeymoon. You'll be ready for some new ones again by then. If Vern hadn't been in such a hurry I would have done your whole trousseau myself.'

Eden almost cringed. Didn't Faith realise Vern wasn't wealthy any more? 'You're very kind,' she murmured helplessly.

'Think nothing of it,' Faith smiled expansively. 'It will give me something to do.'

Eden nodded while the assistant hovered and Faith choose several models for her to try on.

'Island designers are so good,' Faith acknowledged a little later, as she signed a chit for the dresses they had chosen. 'They could compete anywhere in the world.'

Eden gazed with dismay at the pile of clothes and accessories waiting to be packed for them to pick up on their way home. She knew she would be wasting her time to protest any more about wishing to pay for them herself. Trying not to look at the bolt of white silk which Faith was determined to fashion into her wedding dress, she followed her numbly from the shop.

They met Vern for lunch. He chose the fabulous Round Hill where, Eden imagined, almost every famous person ever to visit Jamaica had stayed. The service was fine, the food elegant, a delicious experience, but Eden didn't feel hungry. They had cocktails, fruity drinks spiced with rum, then soup followed by stuffed lobster and a mixture of cool island fruits and icecream, all of which Eden barely tasted. This must be costing Vern a lot of money, and she hoped it was for his aunt's sake rather than hers that he thought it necessary to be so extravagant.

It wasn't until they were drinking the famous Blue Mountain coffee, the coffee grown on the cooler slopes of the ridge of misty mountains which ran like a spine down the length of Jamaica, that Faith left them for a few minutes, giving Eden a chance to speak to Vern alone.

'I don't know how you can talk of being poor,' she exclaimed in a low voice. 'Anyone might be forgiven for thinking exactly the opposite!'

He eyed her coolly. 'Because of this morning?'

She flushed, feeling thoroughly naïve and very defensive. 'I didn't need any clothes. We could easily have been married quietly. It seems insane to be spending so much money.'

Vern sipped his liqueur slowly, his face a grim mask. 'I may not have as much as I used to have,' he said curtly, 'but there are times when a little expenditure is necessary. I don't want my marriage to be a hole-and-corner affair which would embarrass my family and set people talking.'

Eden's face burned. She might have guessed it was his family he was worrying about, not her! Then her anger evaporated as hurt, as usual, took over. 'I was only trying to help,' she said wearily. 'I don't want a hole-and-corner affair any more than you do but we could have compromised. Your aunt spent money this morning as if you were a millionaire. She's one of the nicest persons I've ever met,' Eden hastened, 'but she has obviously no idea of your true circumstances.'

Vern's eyes grew even chillier as he snapped tautly, 'I don't want her to know!'

'She's determined to make my wedding dress, and the material alone was terribly expensive. Not only that,'

Eden faltered unhappily, 'it will mean my going to the plantation almost every day for a fitting.'

'I'll send someone to fetch you.'

Eden could have cried with exasperation. That wasn't the point, and he must know it! If he had loved her it wouldn't have mattered, but she had been looking forward to spending her last days of freedom alone.

'I'm not sure that I'll be able to spare the time,' she prevaricated.

'You'll have to,' he bit out, eyes glittering. As she gazed at him apprehensively, he added, 'If you're worrying over Joe, don't. There's no need. The prospect of having to live by himself doesn't bother him, and he can come to the plantation any time he feels lonely.'

Eden nodded dully.

Vern's voice thickened slightly. 'I'm sure Faith will make a good job of your wedding dress. I'm looking forward greatly to seeing you in it.'

Her breath caught. Because of the way her heart was racing, she said the first thing to enter her head. 'Do you want Jessie to be bridesmaid?'

Vern's mouth hardened with anger. 'You know she'd hate it. Or are you determined to make a public spectacle of her?'

As Eden shrank from his fury, Faith returned, looking very pleased with herself. She didn't appear to notice how white Eden had gone. With a sigh of satisfaction, she settled in her chair again and announced happily,

'I've managed to get Eden an appointment at my favourite place to have her hair done.' When Eden frowned, she smiled apologetically, 'You have beautiful hair, dear, but I think you neglect it. I'll come with you, of course, and explain to the stylist exactly how I want it done to suit the wedding veil I'm making.'

It was after four before they left the town, and by this time Eden scarcely recognised herself. She had long got past the stage of protesting any more over what was being done for her, but she still regarded it as an incredible waste of money.

Vern dropped her off at her house before going home with his aunt, but he arranged to pick both Joe and her up later for dinner. All but one of her new dresses were left in Vern's station wagon. As she was getting married from the plantation, he said it would be better to take them straight there. Eden didn't like to argue with Vern over this as she seemed to have done nothing but disagree with him all day. He assured her he would get one of the maids to unpack them for her and she could check later to see that they were all right, but she didn't think that would be necessary.

He walked with her a little way towards the door, then paused to take hold of her hand. 'You'd better have this,' he said abruptly, with a glance at her startled face, 'otherwise people will begin to wonder.'

He was gone, almost before Eden realised something was glittering on her third finger. In astonishment she saw it was an engagement ring—and a fabulously expensive piece of jewellery, quite unlike the modest earrings he had once given her. Tears rushed to her eyes as she raised it to her lips, not because it was valuable but because she wished with all her heart that Vern had given it to her with love.

Joe was still in a good mood and looking forward to going out, but Eden would rather have stayed at home. She wasn't keen, either, to wear one of the new dresses Vern had bought her before they were married. When he had asked her in Montego Bay to put one aside, she hadn't realised he had meant her to wear it this evening. When she had, he had ignored her unhappy protests as if she had never voiced them.

Regarding the dress stubbornly, as it lay in its silky perfection on her bed, Eden decided impulsively that she would wear her old pink one. Then suddenly she remembered it was torn and she hadn't mended it. Taking it swiftly from her wardrobe, she saw it was ruined beyond redemption. Recalling the frantic way she had thrown it off, that first night of Vern's return, she couldn't really pretend to be surprised.

After showering quickly, she reluctantly put on her new one. She felt impatient that Vern should be so insistent that she smartened herself up, but of course he would want a wife he could at least present to his friends without feeling ashamed of her. Well, he couldn't feel ashamed now, she thought mutinously, staring at her changed image in the mirror. The slender, wide-eyed girl reflected there looked very lovely, with a fragile sophistication which she was sure would appeal to him. He could have no room for complaint, Eden sighed, knowing she would rather have pleased him in other ways.

As he had promised, Vern sent a car for her, and with Joe by her side, Eden didn't have much time to think, but she did try fleetingly to examine the rawness of her emotions. The two terrible years while Vern had been away had dulled them to some extent. No longer did she actually feel she was being torn to pieces. There was a coating of numbness through which odd flashes of feeling occasionally penetrated, and she prayed it would be strong enough to protect her from the ultimate heartache which she suspected she might experience as Vern's wife.

He was coming from the direction of the manager's house as they drew up, and when he saw her his mouth tightened, as if he had drawn a sharp breath. Disregarding his slightly forbidding expression, she asked to speak to him alone, for a moment.

While Joe, with a nod of mistaken understanding, went inside, she quickly drew from her evening purse the roll of notes he had given her, thrusting them into Vern's hands.

'It's money you have to take!' she choked as his eyes hardened. 'When you're my husband I'll wear the clothes you paid for, but I can't do it yet.'

Their eyes clashed across space, hers defiant, his darkening as he stared down at her. Then, muttering something under his breath, he pushed the notes in his pocket.

'Just as you like,' he said coldly, making her feel she had made a great fuss over nothing.

The evening was en famille. Eden didn't know that it would have been a greater ordeal if Vern had invited friends. If it hadn't been for Faith's chatter and Joe—a remarkably well informed conversationalist when he chose to be—she wasn't sure how any of them would have got through it. Vern was aloof, staring at her continually, in obviously a very grim mood, while Jessie's sulky demeanour would have put a damper on any gathering, although Eden was relieved that she wasn't exactly unpleasant.

It was later, after they had finished coffee, when Vern was called to the telephone and Joe was in the hall with Faith, arguing over the authenticity of a painting he admired, that Jessie pounced. Immediately she and Eden were alone she attacked her.

'You can't intend going through with this crazy marriage!' she cried fiercely. 'I know Vern doesn't love you.'

'How can you know?' Eden stammered.

'I can tell!'

So Vern hadn't actually told his sister that. Eden swallowed painfully, supposing it was something. 'Surely you don't mind your brother getting married?' she tried to speak lightly.

Jessie refused to be mollified. 'I don't know how you've managed it,' she raged, 'but if you go ahead and marry him, I promise I'll do everything I can to make your life hell!'

Eden could have retorted that her life had been hell for the past two years. She gazed at Jessie with more than a little bewilderment. It was incredible that she could be so furious with someone for the mistakes she had made herself.

'I wasn't responsible for your accident, Jessie,' she reminded the other girl, refraining, with difficulty, from mentioning Diego Dexter.

'Two years is a long time.' Jessie was tensely defiant. She looked away from Eden as she continued, 'I've forgotten what happened then. The shock of the accident apparently affected my memory, but I do remember some things. I know you were there, that you were driving.'

Eden felt herself grow cold with amazed horror. So this was Jessie's new line—and probably a fairly indisputable one. She wouldn't be the first to pretend amnesia in order to avoid facing a lot of unpleasant facts.

'You were quite rational afterwards,' she said sharply, not bothering to deny Jessie's last accusations.

'I can't remember,' Jessie insisted stubbornly. 'Everything's so vague in my mind—but that's not what I'm bothered about now. I don't know how you've got my brother to agree to marry you, but I don't want you here.'

'I'm afraid there's nothing you can do about it.' Eden had been about to add recklessly, 'Neither can I!' when Vern appeared.

'Vern!' Jessie cried, as though he had arrived in the nick of time to save her from a monster. 'Eden wants me to leave, and she says there's nothing I can do about it!'

Eden gasped as Vern flashed her a murderous glance, swiftly hooded so that Jessie didn't see it. 'I'm sure Eden didn't mean to upset you, Jessie,' he said soothingly. 'It might take a little while to get used to each other, but you need have no fear that anyone's going to upset you, or make you go anywhere you don't want to.'

Jessie finished her act nicely by clutching his hand and pretending to wipe away a tear. 'Oh, darling, she muttered, 'I don't know what I'd do without you!'

Vern released his hand but patted her shoulder affectionately. 'Eden will be here to help. I've often heard you say you'd enjoy having a slave!'

Eden's face went white as again Vern condemned her with another harsh glance over the top of Jessie's bowed head. He might not say so outright, but it was quite clear where his sympathy lay. He would never believe Jessie was deceiving him. There might be a certain irony in knowing that, by not getting rid of her, he was denying his sister what she wanted most. Eden didn't doubt that Jessie's reprisals, because of that, would be vindictive, to say the least. Dully she wondered how Vern could even contemplate marrying someone whom both he and Jessie disliked. The future for all of them, because of this, could be disastrous.

The wedding was arranged for the first Saturday in June, and when the day arrived the sun was shining and there wasn't a cloud in the sky. The only clouds, Eden thought, waking early, were on her own personal horizon. Last night, when Vern had called, his mouth had been a hard, thin line and she had wondered if he was having second thoughts at the last moment. As he left, however, he had merely said he would see her at the ceremony, which didn't suggest he had changed his mind.

Trying not to think of the long hours ahead of her, or the misery of the past weeks, Eden had a shower and put on her shorts. She had seen Vern glancing at them disapprovingly and guessed he would consider them too shabby for his wife to wear. She sighed, for though they were old they were comfortable, and she knew she would have to leave them behind.

Shrugging her thin shoulders, she tried to look on the bright side. Joe was content, the house and land safe, which was all that mattered. She could be happy about that. What happiness she and Vern would find together was another thing.

Jessie had done her best to make her life a misery since the beginning, with her outbursts of temper and hysterics becoming more frequent as the wedding day drew nearer. Eden didn't know what she had said to her aunt, for though Faith had made Eden's wedding dress, her attitude towards her had grown much cooler than it had been on their trip to Montego Bay.

Eden had promised Vern she wouldn't go swimming that morning, but as she slipped from the house and walked along the beach she regretted having given her word. The sea looked inviting and she could have done with a cool dip. Later she wandered back and made Joe some coffee, and after taking it to him began tidying up the house. She felt she must do something to stop herself from worrying over the ordeal in front of her, otherwise she might never find the courage to go through with it.

She had asked Fay to be her bridesmaid—Fay had been delighted. She had even postponed her holiday and Robert was bringing her out to the plantation in time for the wedding in the early afternoon. When Eden had explained to Vern that while Fay was older, she hadn't any close friends of her own age, he had laughed dryly and remarked that as Fay must be about the same age as himself, he thought she would be entirely suitable.

On arriving at the plantation, Eden found Faith waiting to help her to dress. She was amazed at how lovely the house looked as she dodged round a group of florists in the hall. Pausing for a moment, she gazed in wonder, and the workers didn't appear to connect the girl in an old pair of jeans with the bride. There seemed to be flowers everywhere, and several catering vans were standing in the drive. Obviously, as he had said, Vern wasn't allowing a shortage of money to spoil his wedding day!

After the hairdresser had completed her task and applied a little skilful make-up to give colour to Eden's pale cheeks, Faith dismissed her to do the same for Jessie while she helped Eden into her wedding dress. Eden watched, bemused, as Faith zipped her up at the back, at the way the beautiful material clung and billowed around every slender curve of her figure. She couldn't believe it was herself standing in front of the long bevelled mirror looking like a model from a top-class magazine.

'It's wonderful,' she whispered tearfully, as Faith settled the veil on her shining, silky hair. 'You've really done a marvellous job, Aunt Faith, and I'm grateful.'

'You look beautiful!' Faith sighed, her own eyes misty but with the first smile Eden had seen in days. 'Vern will be proud of you.'

Bending her head to hide her sudden despair, Eden huskily thanked her again, then said. 'I'm glad you'll be here with Jessie while we're away.'

They were going sailing for a honeymoon. She hadn't thought they were going to have one, but Vern had told her the evening before that he could spare a weekend.

'The boat's there,' he had shrugged, 'and we can always find a deserted island if we need more space.'

Trying not to think of the last time they had been on a deserted island together, Eden had nodded, trying to copy his indifference, but with Vern feeling as he did about her, she wasn't sure she was looking forward to it.

Faith was saying, 'When Jessie is a little stronger, I'm hoping she'll come back to the States with me. Since my husband died, I guess I'm lonely, and I haven't any children of my own.'

Impulsively Eden hugged her, regardless of her wedding finery. 'I hope you'll always feel this is your home, too. As long as Vern and I are here you'll always be welcome, for as long as you care to stay.'

'Why, honey!' Faith looked quite overwhelmed, her elegant façade a shade shaken. 'You're a nice child, despite ...'

As her voice trailed off in confusion, another one came from the doorway. 'What a touching scene! Is it handkerchiefs all round?'

It was Jessie. While Eden smothered a gasp at her spiteful tone, Faith exclaimed rather loudly, 'Oh, darling, you do look nice!'

'Maybe,' Jessie shrugged, staring at Eden morosely. 'But I'll never be whole and twenty again.'

'Oh, darling!' Faith reiterated helplessly, then, with a little more determination, 'You're still too pretty to let that spoil your day ...'

'And I've still got more sense than my brother!'

Eden stared at Jessie proudly, refusing for once to feel guilty. Who did the Lomaxes think they were, anyway? Both of them blaming her for something she wasn't responsible for.

Faith had taken charge of all the arrangements, and when Mrs Prince called for her advice she hurried off with an almost audible sigh of relief.

The two girls were left alone and Eden said quickly, before Jessie could speak, 'Jessie, couldn't we be friends? If we all have to live together it would be easier for everyone, and I will try and help you.'

Mutinously, Jessie retorted, 'You have to—Vern says so, so you don't have to pretend it's up to you. I'm going to be able to treat you exactly as I like, and you won't be able to do a thing.'

Trying not to shiver at the malice in Jessie's voice, Eden made one last attempt. 'I'm sure you would be happier if you didn't brood so much over the past.'

'It's no use thinking of the future, is it?' Jessie replied tartly. 'Not with a leg like this!' With angry hands she hitched up her long dress, as though determined Eden should see it.

Eden, in spite of feeling startled, took the chance of having a close look at Jessie's leg for the first time. She was surprised to see it was slightly misshapen, but that was all. If Jessie were to leave off her long trousers and skirts and let the sun and air get to it, the faint discoloration might soon disappear, or at least be disguised under the ensuing tan. Very soon, Eden didn't think it would be noticeable at all.

Wisely she decided this might not be a propitious moment to mention that to Jessie. Besides, she imagined it was something her doctors would have already pointed out. Instead she said quietly, 'I don't think your leg looks that bad, and it's not very swollen.'

Jessie's mouth thinned, in a way that reminded Eden of Vern. 'People notice I walk with a limp.'

'A limp can become a habit, you know. Your leg might even be doing it without your knowledge.'

'If that's supposed to be good advice, I don't follow,' Jessie snapped.

Eden said slowly, 'Dad built a patio once, outside our front door. It was really only an extra layer of paving slabs on top of the old ones, but there was no longer a step up to the door. And for days, although I knew it wasn't there, my foot lifted automatically. I believe that, in a slightly different way, might be happening to you.'

For a moment Jessie stared at her, looking, to Eden's astonishment, unusually uncertain, but if Jessie was impressed, she never learnt, because it was then that Faith reappeared, followed by Joe.

'Here's your father, child,' Faith beamed. If she noticed Eden was suddenly shaking, she put it down to last minute nerves.

Joe paused in the doorway, swallowing as he took in the picture his daughter made. He was reacting over-emotionally and not trying to hide it, looking immensely proud of her.

Faith, recognising Jessie's antagonism and Joe's natural loss of control, spoke briskly. 'Now come on, everybody, this will never do, we'll have to get moving! Joe, you'd better give the bride your arm. I have it along the grapevine that Vern's getting mighty restless.'

Eden wanted to run to her father, as she hadn't done since she was small, and beg him to take her home. She wanted to plead with him not to let her marry Vern, but as she watched him and saw how her sudden apprehension brought alarm to his eyes, she knew she could not. Knowing helplessly that her marriage to Vern meant a lot to him and was something she had to go through with, she walked blindly over the room to him and slipped her hand in his.

The service was conducted in a room downstairs, the reception was held in a marquee specially erected in the grounds. Afterwards there was dancing, during which Eden and Vern left, amidst a deluge of confetti, good wishes and slightly ribald if well-meant jokes to begin their honeymoon.

That, Eden thought sombrely, as Vern drove them to where his boat was moored on the coast, was the story of their wedding in a nutshell.

Vern broke the silence, his voice sardonic. 'Enjoy yourself?'

Eden didn't pretend not to know what he was talking about, or to evade the truth. 'Not really.'

'Well,' he laughed curtly, 'there's nothing like being honest.'

'I always try to be.'

He slammed a gear. 'Now you've gone and spoiled things,' he jeered, 'just when I was beginning to feel impressed!'

She looked at him involuntarily. The dark eyes
mocking her were cold. Eden glanced through the
window desolately as they crossed the highway and
plunged towards the coast. What sort of a start was this
to their married life? She couldn't imagine what their
honeymoon was going to be like. In her opinion they
might have been better off at home. If Vern had asked
she might have said so, but she hadn't been asked, she'd
merely been told. Would he always be so dictatorial
with her? she wondered, having an uneasy feeling that
he was starting as he meant to go on.

In other circumstances she would have been thrilled
at the prospect of a sailing honeymoon. She loved the
sea but had never done any real sailing. Just odd trips
which had given her pleasure but no proper experience.
With feelings between Vern and herself so strained, she
didn't think there would be much joy in this trip for
either of them.

When she didn't reply to his last remark, and he
didn't make another, she began thinking of the
wedding. A lot of it was an incredible blur, for being so
recent, but for most of the time she had felt miserable
and frightened. For her father's sake she had tried to
prevent anyone from guessing she was anything but the
proverbially happy bride, and eventually the smile on
her face had seemed to become a fixture.

One part of the afternoon, she suspected, would be
with her indelibly, much as she tried to regard it as
sheer imagination. As Vern had heard the admiring
gasps from the hundreds of guests he had invited, he
had turned, staring at Eden as she approached,
regardless of the sea of faces. There had been something
in his eyes, something she had caught a glimpse of
through the soft swathes of her veiling, but which had
disappeared too swiftly for her to really tell what it was.
It had been something which, while fleeting, had
brought to her heart a quivering joy, but after she had

blinked to make sure she was seeing properly, it had gone.

During the ceremony and the long reception Vern had been so attentive that she had felt again a faint stirring of hope. Now his returning coldness convinced her that he had merely been putting on an act, not for her sake but for the sake of convention.

'Why did you wait so long before telling me we were going away for a few days?' she asked stiffly. If Vern had married someone he loved, she knew he would have been talking about the wedding, perhaps teasing her gently. Eden hated his silence because she was sure it was full of regret, and felt she could put up with it no longer.

He swung down to the cove and the waiting boat. 'I don't have time to explain everything,' he said curtly. 'Learn to think for yourself.'

His voice was so cruel, she shrank from him like a hurt child, wishing she had never spoken. Once started, however, she felt bound to go on. 'A honeymoon wouldn't have mattered. People are bound to find out, sooner or later, that we aren't like a normal married couple.'

'What the hell's that supposed to mean?'

Did he have to snarl? Her cheeks were scarlet, but she retorted stubbornly, 'If you don't feel you have to explain things—well, neither do I!'

'Are you trying to tell me I should follow my own advice?' he asked cynically.

She glanced at the sea, gently blue, and the white tips of the waves breaking on the reefs farther out and trembled. 'If you like.'

Again his eyes mocked her. 'Women have a habit of twisting a man's words, but they can't always do this with his intentions. You'll find, Eden, given time, that ours will be a very normal marriage. And after a while, if you're still worried as to what people believe, we could supply evidence to prove it.'

Eden was sure her whole face was on fire. Unsteadily she scrambled from the truck, which had been necessary because of the roughness of the last few hundred yards of the track. Speechlessly she shook her head, uncaring that Vern must be thinking with satisfaction that he had at last shut her up.

'Be careful!'

Being completely unaware of the deceptive fragility of her slender body, she only heard Vern's teeth snap as she stumbled on the shingle. A man was sitting on the jetty but jumped to his feet when they appeared. He had been looking after the boat until they arrived. Now he would take the truck back to the plantation.

Eden turned to the boat while he exchanged a few words with Vern before leaving. This boat was the same type as Vern had had before, but larger. 'Why did you change it?' she asked curiously, when he joined her.

'Maybe I took a dislike to the other one,' he replied with surprising terseness.

She thought of the other one, her small face very vulnerable as she remembered the happy day they had spent on it. 'I liked it,' she said.

'Well, I didn't,' he snapped, as he helped her on board, his eyes full of glittering impatience when she stiffened, thus making her transition from the jetty to the deck extremely awkward. 'Haven't I told you before, Eden, that the past is dead? It's not a bit of use trying to revive it, and as you killed it yourself, you should be the last to complain!'

CHAPTER SEVEN

ON the boat they were alone at last after what seemed to Eden to have been a very long day. Determined that Vern shouldn't guess how badly he could hurt her, she blinked the tears from her eyes before glancing at him enquiringly. It would only irritate and goad him if she burst into tears every time he spoke sharply.

Interpreting her glance correctly, he said coldly, 'You can go below and make some tea, if you like, while I get under way.'

'Where are we going?' she asked tentatively.

'As far as possible before dark.'

Again no real answer, although in this case, Eden realised he probably couldn't give one. Distances in the Caribbean were immense and many of the tiny islands had no names.

The galley was small but completely up to date. While the kettle boiled she did a brief tour of inspection. In the other, much larger cabin were two bunks which could be used as seats during the day, and through a door, across a passage, was a minute bathroom with a shower. She tried not to view the bunk beds with a sigh of relief, for clearly they were never designed for double occupancy.

Her cheeks hot, Eden returned to the galley, wishing she could get over the childish habit of blushing. She wasn't a child any more. On her next birthday she would be twenty-one, and during the past two years she had suffered so much from her emotions that she couldn't be anything else but totally adult. Sexually she might still be completely innocent, but in every other way she was grown up.

Bitterly she wondered how her love for Vern could, in the circumstances, have grown stronger instead of weaker. And why before, when it had been such a warm happy feeling, it now seemed to be tearing her apart. She didn't want him to touch her this evening, for she couldn't be sure what her reactions would be. She didn't think he would, but he was unpredictable, and this part of the world bred men of strong passions. If he attempted to make love to her—Eden's cheeks grew hotter than ever with uncertainty and tension, she might never be able to resist him, and she was desperately afraid that she might unconsciously betray her feelings for him.

Reflecting anxiously on this, Eden made two mugs of tea when the kettle boiled and carried them on deck. At the plantation they had both changed into light pants and shirts, to save them changing again on the boat. The sun was still hot and Eden felt her clothes sticking to her and wished she had worn something even cooler.

Vern accepted his tea with a brief word of thanks and she wondered, as his glance went over her, what he was thinking. Quickly she averted her eyes from the brown strength of his throat in the open neck of his shirt, the grim set of his mouth.

Taking a quick gulp of tea, she felt her heart sink when he said, 'Jessie looked better today. She seems more interested in Martin Darel.'

Eden didn't want to be reminded of the Darels. Throughout the afternoon she had been frequently aware of Carita's dagger-like glances, the other girl making no attempt to hide the contempt she felt for the girl Vern had married.

'I'm sure Jessie will be fine, given time,' she murmured vaguely. 'Martin's a nice man.'

'If you leave him alone.'

Eden frowned. 'If you're talking about the first time we met, he was just curious.'

'And encouraged!'

His mouth twisted in a cynical smile, and Eden sighed. She hated Vern in this mood. It emphasised the barrier between them, which seemed to be growing more insurmountable in every way. She made a rather obvious attempt to change the subject.

'I didn't realise,' she commented, 'that you knew so many people. There were a lot of guests.'

'Yes,' Vern replied tersely, slanting her a derisive glance.

'Did—did you think I looked nice in the dress your aunt made?' she persisted, remembering him remarking that he was looking forward to seeing her in it.

'You looked very nice,' he agreed, his eyes narrowed against the sinking sun on a shimmering sea.

She gave up, if not without another sigh which he didn't—or pretended he didn't—hear. She might as well go back down below and hold a conversation with herself about the wedding. It could be less wearing! Aware that he was eyeing her mockingly, she asked dully. 'What time will you want dinner?'

'Will I want dinner?' he countered sardonically, putting his cup down and pulling her into his arms so swiftly she had no chance of avoiding him. Her own cup hit the deck with a clatter as she dropped it, and she thought wildly, as his mouth descended, that it was a good job it had been empty.

Her lids fluttered as Vern's mouth touched hers, lightly at first, then with deepening pressure. Although the bodily contact sent fierce currents tingling through her, she might have broken free if his arms hadn't tightened. She could feel the heat from his body and the pressure of his hard lips playing havoc with her powers of resistance.

Then, as suddenly as he had taken hold of her, he was pushing her away, making her realise he had kissed her deliberately to increase her nervousness, should she have any, over what was to happen later.

'My apologies,' he rasped, deepening her suspicions. 'I imagine you're trying to keep my mind on food!' As she rubbed a speechless hand over her bruised mouth and nodded angrily, she could see he was enjoying himself coolly. 'You'd better make something for about nine,' he said, turning his attention to the boat again. 'I'll drop anchor then for the night.'

There wasn't enough to do to keep her occupied for hours, so after she had prepared the steak ready to cook and washed the salad, Eden found a new pair of shorts and with the top of a bikini, went back on deck to sunbathe.

She felt Vern's head swivel to watch her as she unrolled a sleeping bag she had found and tried to relax on it against the rail. Feeling his eyes on her made her remember how he had kissed her, and she wished he would look the other way.

'Why aren't you wearing the bottom half?' she heard him asking idly, as she huddled on her stomach, staring at the sea. 'Why just the top half of your bikini?'

'Because I thought my legs were bare enough!' she muttered recklessly, then hoped that his ears weren't nearly as good as his eyes.

'They're certainly tantalising,' he teased, leaving her in no doubt as to the efficiency of his hearing. 'Another time, though, when I'm not so busy, I'd be interested to learn why you felt it necessary to consider my reactions.'

Her eyes jerked in alarm towards him, to find him grinning, with a one-step-ahead-of-you expression on his face. Inexplicably, as their eyes met, his own sobered, and with a strange, hunted feeling beginning inside her, Eden buried her face in her arms with a hollow groan.

Later she cooked their dinner. When it was almost ready she went to tell him, having heard the engines stop several minutes ago. They were anchored in a bay, off an island, a grey and green mass in the fading light. It wasn't the same island she had visited with him before, but it looked incredibly beautiful.

Of Vern there was no sign, but as she noticed the pile of clothes on the deck, she realised he must have gone for a swim. Suddenly she knew he hadn't bothered with his swimming trunks and, in some confusion, retreated below again. At this rate she'd soon feel like a Jack-in-the-box! she thought fretfully.

Shortly afterwards, when Vern joined her, her suspicions were confirmed. He was carrying his clothes with only an old towel draped round his waist.

'I'll be with you in a minute,' he said, disappearing into the other cabin.

When he returned, he was wearing a fresh shirt and trousers and, as she had everything served, he sat down beside her. 'Umm, this smells good,' he smiled, looking at the steak with appreciation.

To keep herself from concentrating on how good Vern looked, Eden asked about the island.

'Tomorrow,' he promised, 'we'll go ashore. There's an old house there, although I don't believe it belongs to anyone. We can explore.'

The meal was cooked to perfection and Vern produced a bottle of wine. As he uncorked it carefully, Eden glanced at him warily. 'I've made up the beds in the other cabin.'

'One would have done.'

All the time they ate she wondered anxiously what he meant. Perhaps he intended sleeping on deck. She had changed into a silky dress. It was just a short one, but it left her arms and shoulders bare and she suddenly realised he might think she had put it on deliberately to attract him. Immediately she regretted the jingling bangles on her wrists, the gold-coloured chain round her slim neck. They had only been cheap, but she had been unable to resist wearing them. In the other cabin she had thought the whole effect very nice, but now, with Vern's eyes returning to her contemplatively again and again, she began feeling like some fifth-rate chorus girl.

'Your cooking is superb, Eden, I'll say that for you.' With a sigh of satisfaction he pushed his empty plate aside and reached for the percolater.

Eden tried not to notice how his tone implied that this was all he could commend about her. 'Thank you,' she murmured.

'Where did you get your necklace?' he asked idly, as they drank their coffee.

'Montego Bay,' she replied guardedly, her eyes widening. 'It—it was my own money.'

'I wasn't asking that,' he said curtly, leaning nearer to slide his fingers under it, so that she felt the weight of his hand against her breast.

Swallowing, in a way she knew he must notice, she tried to remain still while he purported to examine it. Just when she was beginning to think he was taking an unconscionably long time over it, he took his hand away abruptly.

'I'm glad you like it,' she choked.

His brows lifted, but he let her comment pass as he narrowly surveyed her tired face. 'Are you going to bed yet? It's getting late.'

Realising it was, she nodded and began stacking their dishes. She thought he might tell her to leave them, but he merely said, 'You wash, I'll dry.' When they were finished, and she said hastily, 'Goodnight, Vern,' he nodded but didn't actually reply.

'Would you like to use the bathroom first?' she asked from the doorway, feeling she might be unreasonable in trying to keep it all to herself.

'Good idea.' He walked past her. 'Kind of you to think of it.'

Hoping he wasn't being sarcastic, Eden waited until

he came out. When he did, he was wearing a short silk robe and, she suspected, nothing underneath. 'Do you want anything else?' she managed, as he paused beside her.

'Only you,' he drawled, taking her in his arms.

The breath seemed to leave Eden's body. 'You can't mean it?' she gasped.

'Not right at this moment,' he laughed at her obvious discomfiture. 'Go and get in bed.'

As she broke from his arms, he made no effort to hold her. His eyes were taunting and she guessed he was only trying to frighten her. Gathering up her nightclothes, she went to the bathroom, trying to stop worrying over his exact intentions. She didn't think she was in any real danger. He liked to make her believe he was going to make love to her while all along he would rather die than do so. He loathed her too much.

The shower was warm and helped her to relax. She wished she could stay there for ever, letting the soft flow of water soothe the tenseness from her limbs. It hadn't occurred to her until now that alone, on board the boat, she was completely at Vern's mercy and had no one to help her, no matter what he did.

After drying quickly on a big, soft towel, she slipped on one of her new nighties. She hadn't dared bring her old pyjamas, after what Vern had said about her shorts. Now she wished she had. The nightdress was low-cut and sexy. Faith had asked a salesgirl in one of the shops they had gone to to choose Eden half a dozen. Glancing at the minimal coverage the one she was wearing provided, she was relieved that Vern wouldn't see her in it. Although he threatened obliquely, she had come to the conclusion that he would never make her his wife in the true sense of the word. More probably, she decided bleakly, he would wait until he was sure Joe couldn't get the land back, then divorce her.

Vern must have heard the slight noise she made

getting into bed, for he came in before she could put the light out. As she glanced at him in nervous surprise, he sat down on the side of her bunk. She drew a sharp breath as she saw his eyes darken with desire as he firmly pulled the sheet from her defensively clutching hands.

'I thought I could wait,' he stated baldly, his glance sweeping over her. 'Where you're concerned, my will power isn't what it should be. You're too enticing.'

Leaning over, he took her in his arms, as he had done a few minutes ago, but this time with no indication that he meant to release her. While she gazed at him in a kind of frozen horror, he ran his hands over her shoulders, down her arms, then around her back, lifting her towards him to meet his seeking mouth.

It was the first brush of his lips that released Eden from the trance she was in. 'No!' she cried, then faltered, 'Please, Vern, you said you'd wait!'

'I didn't say how long,' he muttered thickly, pressing soft kisses from the side of her mouth to her ear. 'I paid enough, didn't I?'

'Paid?' She struggled against him, her heart beating frantically.

'You can't complain.' He stilled her struggles harshly, while he was speaking. 'You've had quite a lot already.'

Her slender, artist's fingers found the angle of his hard jaw as she tried to push him away. How could he even think of making love to her in such a coldblooded way? She wouldn't have thought it possible. If he did— a shudder ran through her as she was suddenly convinced he might—he might be even more bitter in the morning. For his sake as well as her own, she must try and make him see sense.

'You'll live to regret it if you don't stop,' she warned breathlessly.

He merely laughed, and instead of retreating from the thrust of her hand, turned his mouth against her soft palm. As feeling rushed through her, he lifted his head to note her hot cheeks. 'I could regrèt it more if I didn't,' he said. 'You would only turn to other men.'

'There haven't been other men!' she retorted desperately. 'You must know that.'

'I know nothing of the sort,' he jeered, obviously not intending to give an inch. 'Diego Dexter, for one, wouldn't be seen within miles of a virgin. His affairs are legend, but he drew the line at that. He had no use for women without experience.'

'Well, he never had me!'

'You say that so convincingly,' he mocked. 'What a pity I'm not the sort to be taken in by a pair of innocent blue eyes.'

'I'm not trying to deceive you!'

'You can even manage a few tears!'

Was she crying? Eden was startled to discover she was and shrank from the contemptuous face above her. If only she could concentrate on his hate and her own anger and still the wild flutter of her pulses. Every time his mouth touched her she felt off balance and an increasing desire to give in to him.

'Leave me alone,' she whispered, a plea which he totally disregarded.

As if tiring of their previous conversation, he buried his face in her neck. 'I'm glad you aren't wearing too many clothes,' she could feel him beginning to smile coolly as he nuzzled her warm skin, 'just enough to tantalise a man.'

'I didn't choose my nightdress,' she stammered, again trying to push him away. He was near, yet not too near. There must still be time to reason with him. Desperately she tried to think of something really sensible to say to him, which would make him think twice about going any farther.

'Your nightdress is very nice,' he muttered, raising his head as his hand slid to her breast, 'but I'd rather see you without it.'

'No!' she cried in alarm, wondering fearfully if it wasn't already too late for the words of wisdom which were curiously evading her.

'I want you, Eden,' he said, very slowly and distinctly, making sure she understood. 'I didn't plan this, but you'd better know, while I can still talk rationally, that there's no way you can escape your obligations.'

'Without love?' she asked bitterly, meaning his.

He obviously thought she was speaking of herself. 'Some women aren't capable of it,' he retorted curtly. 'But don't worry, your body might be enough. And from now on,' he warned, 'until I tire of it, it's going to be my exclusive property.'

As if to emphasise that he meant to stake his claim, he lay down beside her, his long legs stretching the length of the bunk.

'There's not room!' she cried out in fright.

'I've managed on less,' he taunted, and she could have wept when she remembered how gentle he had once been. Two years ago she was certain he would never have spoken to her with such insolence in his voice.

She tried to fight him, avoiding his mouth, for she knew what that could do to her, but he was too strong for her. 'Let go of me!' she choked, twisting and turning.

His arms tightened as she struggled to escape him, then, when she was completely exhausted, he gave a grunt of sober satisfaction and levered himself up on one elbow. Taking hold of the sheet, he pulled it from her, then, grasping her nightdress, drew it ruthlessly over her head. As she heard it rustle on to the floor behind him, Eden's heartbeats were so loud she thought he must hear them.

He was staring down on her, his cheeks dully flushed, his eyes almost black as his glance fell on the soft rounded curves of her figure. She gazed back at him, and it was like a moment suspended in time while he slowly lowered his head.

'No,' she whispered, her eyes closing gently in instinctive surrender.

If she had really meant to go on resisting him it was too late. His mouth was suddenly on hers, she could feel the warm inner moisture gliding over her skin, and he was holding her slender body prisoner by the weight of his own. She heard him make a rough sound in his throat as he began kissing her, and all the rational thoughts she had been putting together to present him with fled.

As his mouth crushed hers, Eden was so dazed by the hot pressure of his long kisses that she didn't notice him shrugging out of his robe. Her eyes flew open only as she felt him beside her, as naked as she was.

'Oh, please . . .' she moaned.

'I've wanted you in my arms like this for so long it's been driving me mad,' he said thickly, his mouth closing urgently over her trembling lips.

While his mouth explored hers sensuously, with one hand tilting her chin, his other stroked her slender limbs and soft breasts. Eden's breath caught as he gently caressed their tender fullness and pink peaks. Helplessly her arms went around his neck and tightened as feeling mounted between them. She had never known anything like the deep, erotic sensation he was arousing, and the world and everyone in it but themselves vanished beneath the clamouring hunger of her body.

She was suddenly on fire with responses so deep they seemed to be wrenching her to pieces. She began twisting restlessly, small moans escaping her while her hands curled and uncurled in unsated passion. She was shaking, her face buried against him, her heart beating with a slow, heavy excitement.

Vern's arms tightened fiercely as he felt her slender

body shuddering as her hunger for him increased. Rolling over, he pulled her swiftly under him, his breath coming in rough gasps which the blood pounding in her ears prevented her from hearing, nor was she entirely conscious of his heavy legs parting her trembling limbs. She wasn't aware that he had reached the point of no return. If she had been she couldn't have protested as his exploring hands threatened to drive her insane, until her body arched wilfully against his, as if pleading for release.

If Eden had been floating on a cloud, Vern's somewhat brutal possession of her brought her swiftly down to earth again. He hurt her badly, and afterwards, hearing him assuring her it was her own fault made her feel even more miserable. She might have tried to understand that it had been too late for him to stop if his harsh voice had contained any remorse, but while in the dim light of the cabin, his face had looked pale, she hadn't seen any signs of real regret on it.

Sobbing, she pushed him from her, even when he told her thickly to lie still.

'It will be better next time,' he said in a tone which somehow suggested to Eden's growing apprehension that the next time might not be so far away.

'Eden,' he murmured, confirming her suspicions, 'why not have a rest? Then in a few minutes, when you're feeling better, I can show you how wonderful it can be.'

'How can you say that!' she cried fiercely, her small face white and tormented. 'It was one of the worst experiences of my life!'

She hadn't meant it. She couldn't forget the rapture, but what followed had been in the nature of a major disappointment. She had a feeling that she wasn't normal. That she had let them both down. 'I hate you!' she cried, reaction setting in heavily.

Immediately his expression hardened. 'If I'd thought it was the first time for you, I needn't have hurt you—at least not as much as I did.'

'I told you!' Her small fists beat a hysterical tattoo on his chest.

'You did,' he agreed grimly, 'but it wasn't my fault that I didn't believe you. The evidence was all against you, you have to admit.'

'You decided it was.'

He ignored that. 'I can only conclude that you've been a promiscuous little tease. You might be grateful, once you've cooled down, that it was your husband who called your bluff. Surely,' he asked, his eyes glittering over her, 'you didn't expect to get away with it for ever, did you? You might have come off even worse with another I could name.'

Was it possible? As she woke slowly from a drugged sleep, the eventual outcome of silent weeping, Eden found her eyes wandering dazedly across to the other bunk. Vern was there, he had refused to sleep elsewhere, although she sensed he had got no more rest than she had. He was sleeping now, his face turned towards her, and she couldn't get rid of the feeling that he was watching her, even with his eyes closed.

Because she couldn't stop watching him, she decided to get up and take a shower. When she returned from the bathroom he was gone, and she guessed he would be swimming. She wished she had thought of that, too, as she quickly found a pair of shorts and a sleeveless top. A dip in the sea might have done more for her this morning than standing under a shower.

Brushing her thick hair, she glanced wryly in the mirror, wondering why the glowing smoothness of her face reflected none of the ordeal she had endured the night before. A warm colour rose in her cheeks as she remembered how she had felt in Vern's arms. Quickly she put her brush down and almost raced to the galley.

If she began cooking breakfast it might prevent her from thinking too much. The beds could wait until later.

She didn't feel hungry, but she knew Vern would be. Frowning, she wondered what he would have to say to her when he came in. It mightn't be anything pleasant, not after the way she had rejected his efforts to console her a few hours ago, but she should be getting used to the wounding things he came out with by now.

She had bacon fried and coffee perking when she heard him climbing back on board. Five minutes later he came into the galley, fully dressed, only the dampness of his hair betraying what he had been doing.

'That smells good,' he said quietly.

His gentle approach, seeming as it did to mock the defences she had erected, confused Eden. Glancing at him uncertainly, she said quickly, 'I thought you'd be hungry.'

'I am,' his eyes went over her, as if there was something which interested him more than food. He took his time studying her slender figure, her smooth young face and shining hair. 'You look like a million dollars this morning,' he said. Then, not quite so sardonically, 'Do you feel all right?'

He looked so fit, although he was still pale under his tan. Because she would rather not notice such things, Eden turned sharply away from him.

'Yes.' She placed bacon and sausages with kidneys and eggs on a plate and handed it to him angrily, but almost spoiling the effect by nearly grinning when he exclaimed 'Ouch!' because the plate was hot. 'Coffee ready and toast coming up,' she added, with a little more satisfaction.

'Thank you.' He sat down, his mouth tightening.

'You don't need to worry that I shan't be able to cook!' she rejoined tartly.

'Eden!' his eyes glittered, 'that's not what I meant.'

Her face growing hot, she begged, 'Please, I'd rather not talk about it.'

He sighed, hesitated, as if counting ten, then picked up his fork again. 'We have to some time, you know.'

'There—there's nothing to talk about!' she replied fearing that if he persisted she might burst into tears. She hadn't thought there would be any left, now she suspected there might be.

She saw his knuckles whiten around the fork he was holding, but to her great relief he changed the subject.

'I thought we might visit the island this morning. If we only took a packet of sandwiches, we could leave straight away and cook an enormous dinner when we come back.'

Eden packed a flask of coffee and another of a cool drink while Vern cut the sandwiches. She was surprised at his neat efficiency as he trimmed them and wrapped them up. For a big man he moved very quickly and seemed to have absolute control over every inch of his lean, powerful body. She caught herself watching him closely. In repose his face wore a grim expression and she wondered if he was regretting their hasty marriage already. She couldn't forget what he had said the previous evening about her being his property until he tired of her.

He treated her gently that morning, but he was far from solicitous. Whatever they were doing, he kept his eye on her without getting too close. Eden began to feel less threatened and relaxed under the benign influence of sea and sun and complete solitude. Very occasionally she even managed to forget Vern was there.

They explored the island thoroughly, but there wasn't much to see. It was craggy with plenty of trees to provide a welcome shade, and they found a small stream running down from one of the higher hills. There were a lot of birds and the lush undergrowth seemed alive with the scurrying of small animals.

Vern pointed out almond and banana trees while Eden spotted a coconut palm and several others, all growing wild.

'I can't recall anyone living here,' Vern mused, as they reached a spot from which they could view the whole island and looked around. 'It's fairly obvious that someone, at some time or another, has tried to start a plantation here. I doubt if it will be in any records, but I wonder why they gave up.'

On the way down, Eden picked some oranges and lemons to take back to the boat and Vern showed her a group of pimento trees which, he said, might support his theory that the island had once been inhabited. The leaves of the pimento tree smelt of cloves and were marketed as allspice, which had once been known as Caribbean gold.

As they circled the shore, on the opposite side of the island to where the boat was moored, they came across a derelict homestead. It was so overgrown by trees and creepers that from the sea it would be impossible to know it was there.

'You must be right,' Eden exclaimed, glancing at Vern. 'What a wonderful place to live. I wonder who it belonged to?'

'Someone who has obviously abandoned it,' he remarked dryly. 'You probably like it because it reminds you of where you used to live, bang on the beach.'

'Yes, of home,' she agreed, her eyes suddenly misty.

'For heaven's sake, Eden,' he bit out, so savagely he startled her, 'you can't be homesick already! Can I rely on you not to burst into tears if I remind you that your father's house isn't your home any more?'

Eden glanced at him quickly, jerked from the dreamy, sun-induced mood she had been in. The shirt Vern wore covered his broad chest and shoulders while his khaki shorts did nothing to hide the hard strength of his long legs. He looked stern and somehow menacing, and she thought bitterly that she wouldn't dare shed even a single tear!

Trying to swallow the lump in her throat, she followed the rigid line of his back, back to the dinghy in which they had come ashore. 'Let's have a swim before lunch,' he suggested, as if the cool silence between them had never been.

The water was deep and clear and just the right temperature to make swimming a delight. 'Tomorrow,' Vern promised, as they waded ashore again, 'we'll bring some snorkelling equipment. There are some reefs farther out which might prove interesting?'

So they weren't going home straight away. As she gleaned this from Vern's remark, Eden wasn't sure whether to be glad or sorry. Each hour they spent alone was bringing as much torment as pleasure. She kept having insane inclinations to touch him and had constantly to remind herself that this could prove very dangerous. If she treated him coolly, he might continue keeping his distance, but if she encouraged him to believe he was attractive to her, she would only have herself to blame for the consequences.

Vern carried their lunch to a shady spot under some trees, where they could have a table of soft grass instead of sand. They hadn't bothered to put on their shorts again as he said they could have another swim before returning to the boat.

'We're dry already,' he shrugged, 'and it's too hot for clothes.'

Because he was so impersonal, and she was so used to practically living in a bikini at home, she didn't argue. Having eaten no breakfast, she was ravenous, her mind shamelessly concentrating on food. They hadn't brought many sandwiches, and she sighed ruefully as she spread out the cloth she had popped in the bag containing the flasks. She didn't try to suppress an exclamation of surprised delight when she saw Vern unpacking a chicken from the icebox.

'Ha!' It seemed he couldn't suppress a grin either, when he noticed her almost mentally licking her lips. 'Does this appeal to you, you greedy child? One of Mrs Prince's specials you didn't see me put in.'

'Oh, scrumptious!' Eden felt so pleased she forgave him calling her a child. Chicken, anyhow, was a rare treat. She hadn't been Vern's wife long enough to be used to such things and already her mouth was watering.

'I noticed you ate no breakfast,' he shot her a stern glance. 'I wonder you've lasted so long. I've been half prepared to find you fainting all morning.'

She felt suddenly breathless as his eyes raked over her, seeming to be asking if she remembered things she would rather forget. 'I—I wasn't hungry then,' she mumbled weakly, her heart pounding.

Vern turned again to the icebox, producing buttered rolls and a bottle of wine. As Eden's eyes positively rounded, he said solemnly, 'Didn't you know you'd married a very clever man?'

Eden glanced at him, about to toss back a similarly teasing remark, when she suddenly found she couldn't Vern was just joking, but no one, she knew, would doubt his intellect. What would he say, she wondered, if she were to tell him that if only he had loved her she could have lived with him on an island like this for ever and never cared whether he was clever or not!

CHAPTER EIGHT

LATER, replete with good food and wine, it seemed the most natural thing in the world to fall asleep. Long past midday, it was still very warm and the heat, combined with the exercise she had taken, caused Eden to lie back on the grass and close her eyes. When she woke she found herself in Vern's arms.

Everything was quiet and still; even the trees over their heads had no motion, giving her a feeling she was still dreaming. Vern's face swam hazily above her own and the grass was soft, like a bed. She felt relaxed and utterly content.

Vern brushed the tumbled hair back from her forehead, the slow movement of his fingers doing nothing to unduly disturb her. When he saw her eyelids flicker, he murmured, 'Still tired?'

She wondered if he had been sleeping too. He always looked fresh and vital, even at the end of a busy day. 'No,' she answered his question with a dreamy smile, not yet completely aware of how close he was holding her.

He hesitated only a moment when she didn't repulse him before beginning to kiss her, and her face flamed as she suddenly came wide awake and realised what was happening. By not pushing him immediately away, she must have invited it, and it was up to her to stop it before it went too far. Vern had married her for his own reasons, all the wrong reasons, and she would be mad to give in to him. He hated her, and because in some small way he still found her attractive, he meant to exorcise this attraction by making love to her. It was what was known as getting it out of one's system.

Knowing this, as his mouth trailed over her cheek,

Eden gasped, 'No!' and compressed her lips.

'Open your mouth, Eden.'

She tried to resist, but his arms tightened around her and she felt she was on fire as she was drawn fiercely against the masculine toughness of his body. Her eyes closed again as his hands became incredibly persuasive, moulding the softness of her rounded curves, skimming skilfully over her slender limbs until she became aware that he was deviously arousing urgent feelings. She felt ready to melt as his lips sought hers ruthlessly and made no further attempt to keep her own closed.

He went on kissing her, his mouth filled with hungry passion, his heart hammering strongly over hers, and despite suspecting he was seducing her deliberately, Eden found it impossible to resist him. Everything was slipping away. She wanted nothing other than to stay in his arms, to let him satisfy the rush of desperate longing that came over her. Her mind, in any case, appeared to have lost its battle with her body. As he kissed her, she found herself clinging to him eagerly, her body betraying what she hadn't the immediate courage to put in words, that she might go crazy if he didn't make love to her.

'Eden!' she heard his smothered groan as her shaking hands ran over his hard chest. Like a man defeated he tugged at the ties of her bikini before tearing it off. Then he lowered his mouth to her breast, taking no notice of her gasping protests as he took possession of a rosy nipple.

The shock was so great that she cried out in terror. It might have been the first time he had touched her, it all seemed so new. Then, as he persisted and his hand slid slowly down over her stomach, she whimpered again as flames spread through her, down her limbs, up her spine. She felt sensation rushing along her veins in a fiery flood and knew instinctively that the same fire was enveloping him.

He raised himself from her for a second, throwing off his trunks, and, as Eden felt every nerve in her body screaming, his hair-roughened chest was crushing her breast, their mouths meeting again in wild desire.

'You aren't frightened?' he groaned thickly, his lips moving to her ear in quick, fevered kisses. 'I want you so much.'

'Oh, no, Vern—I don't know,' she breathed, 'Just please love me . . .'

'You're sure?'

She felt a tremor running through him as she nodded and instantly all her lingering fears dissolved in a flame of mutual passion. She heard his groan of capitulation as his body hardened and he moved to make her completely his.

In the moment of possession, she expected to be hurt again, as she had been the night before. It wasn't a fully conscious thought, as the fever burning along her veins made rational thought impossible, but amazingly there was no pain. Any fleeting apprehension was quickly gone, and she clung to him mindlessly as ripples of sensation mounted and spiralled between them. Her arms curved round his neck and she cried out his name as his lips plundered her full, throbbing breasts while the passion welding them together grew overwhelmingly. A tide of burning sweetness seemed to turn her body into molten fire beneath him as he caressed her to fever-pitch. Then everything changed. Whereas before she had felt she was floating, she suddenly found the feeling inside her exploding in a blaze of dazzling light as he brought her to the ultimate shuddering peak of surrender. He demanded and she gave as he buried his lips in her throat and a final spasm of rapture engulfed them.

He held her shaking body in his arms so long afterwards, she thought he wasn't going to let her go. It wasn't until several minutes had passed that he left her, with a deep sigh to get dressed. Dazed, Eden lay in the stillness, the air moving softly over her nakedness, where only moments before Vern had been. Unashamedly she watched as he dragged his shorts over strong brown limbs, but suddenly shivered as he began packing up the remains of their picnic lunch.

He looked so stern, she wished she didn't remember so clearly how they had been—fast in each other's arms, limbs entwined, lips touching passionately. Last night he might have hurt her, but this afternoon he had given her a glimpse of heaven. Scarcely realising what she was doing, she got to her feet and went over to kiss him gratefully on his cheek.

It must have been a mistake, because he jerked away. His eyes glittering with dislike, he thrust her from him. 'What was that for?' he asked, almost brutally.

It was like a slap on the face. She positively reeled, but managed to falter dully, 'I'm sorry.'

'Never mind,' he said coolly, confusing her entirely by averting his glance from her. 'It's getting late. We'd better be getting back to the boat.'

Numbly she nodded as he picked up the empty containers and started walking towards the beach. Hastily she scrambled into her own clothes and followed.

Vern made love to her again that night, again raising her to blissful heights, but afterwards he returned to the other bunk. Eden knew it was probably her own fault that he left her so abruptly, for she hadn't let him touch her willingly. It wasn't that she disliked his lovemaking; with burning cheeks she admitted to herself the pleasure it now gave her. But while she acknowledged that, everything inside her cried out against being taken in cold blood.

She couldn't challenge him with it, though, for she had known all along that he didn't love her, but she was coming to hate his silent contempt. She could almost feel it moving in him when he held her in his arms. Whether it was directed against her or himself, she wasn't sure, but she always knew it was there. He never spoke when he was making love to her. As his passion mounted he might murmur unintelligibly against her lips, but this was purely physical. He never revealed by word or deed that he loved her.

Because she was so overwrought, Eden snapped at him next morning when she woke to find him sitting on the edge of her bed with only a towel around his waist. With all her senses clamouring traitorously in seconds, she had to clench her hands tightly to prevent them from stealing out to him. More hours such as they had shared yesterday might soon have her blurting out that she loved him, and she suddenly suspected that might be what he was aiming at. The ultimate victory with which to mock her.

'No!' she gasped as he leant over her, a grim smile on his mouth as he traced her face with fingers still tangy with the salty freshness of the sea.

His brows lifted, a more tolerant glint in his eyes. 'You aren't properly awake. Tomorrow morning you must come swimming with me, then we can stay in bed all day.'

'No!' she cried again, aware that her willpower might never be strong enough to resist it.

'No?' His eyes darkened sardonically. 'Be sure you know what you're rejecting, my girl. I never press my attention where it isn't wanted, and you could soon be feeling extremely deprived.'

She had a suspicion he was taunting her a little but how could she back down after that? He was implying that once she had belonged to him she couldn't do without him.

'I won't be treated like a—a sex object!' she retorted wildly.

'Suit yourself!' He rose, whipping off his towel as he

slammed out of the cabin, leaving her thinking despairingly of the moments of rapture which might have been hers if she hadn't spoken so hastily.

They spent a week sailing and swimming and just lying around in the sun. Vern did a lot of fishing, although he didn't appear to take it very seriously. Usually he threw most of his catch back into the sea. The sea was alive with all sorts of fish, including the really big ones. Vern told her of some of his adventures, fishing for barracuda, but she was more interested in the smaller specimens which swam among the reefs.

Vern didn't attempt to make love to her again, or even kiss her, and she soon began to realise what he meant when he'd talked of her feeling deprived. Sometimes the longing to be in his arms was so great that it took a great effort to restrain herself from throwing herself at him. If this form of deprivation bothered him, he didn't show it, and Eden envied him his continuing remoteness.

The evening before they were due home, she turned to him desperately after dinner, her face pale, because it hadn't been an easy day. They had spent most of the time snorkelling, and having him so near her, underwater, for hours had affected her badly. She had a feeling that if he kept his distance much longer it might drive her mad.

'Vern,' she faltered unevenly,' her own words startling her slightly, 'you have no need to be jealous of other men. There weren't any . . .'

'Jealous?' His brows rose superciliously.

'Oh, please!' She was terribly strung up and failing to hide it—the fear that he had misunderstood not helping. 'That wasn't what I meant, honestly! I just thought you might believe I'd been promiscuous.'

'I could hardly believe that now,' he said dryly, meeting her worried glance. 'I don't think I'm even convinced of the other men any more. I imagine you were just beginning to feel your power and experimenting, which wouldn't be so difficult to forgive.'

'Then why . . .?'

As she hesitated unsteadily, he regarded her coolly, refusing to make things easier for her. 'Why what?'

'Why do you dislike me so much?'

Because her cheeks were scarlet, he must have guessed what she was really trying to say, but he gave no hint. 'If I dislike you,' he rapped out, 'it's not so much because of other men as because of Jessie. Do you expect me to forget what you did to her? Experimenting is one thing, deliberate cruelty leading to near disaster quite another!'

Eden stared at him. He was grim-faced, his mouth a straight hard line, his brows frowning above cold green eyes.

'Vern?' she took a step towards him then stopped. She had felt tempted, for a moment, to tell him the truth but again she realised he might not believe her. And if he did—the thought halted her, he might have no compunction about throwing his sister out. Beneath his urbane exterior, Eden guessed, lay a man who could be absolutely ruthless when he chose. He could be frightening when he was merely angry, his ice-cold brand of anger being much more frightening than that of those who ranted and raved. Jessie might never rally after it, because she loved her brother. No, if the truth was ever told it had to come from Jessie. Eden had told herself this a hundred times, each time becoming more sure she was right. 'I'm sorry,' she whispered painfully, since there seemed nothing more to say.

His shoulders lifted in cynical acceptance as he turned his back on her.

How she was to fill in her time in her new home worried Eden. She doubted that Jessie would keep her busy the whole of each day and she had never been used to sitting around doing nothing, although she liked to relax in the evening. They returned to Jamaica late the next afternoon, and while they waited for the truck which would take them back to the plantation she plucked up enough courage to ask Vern about it.

'You're to help Jessie.' He glanced at her briefly.

'I'm sure she won't want me all day.'

'If you must kill yourself,' he managed to convey that as far as he was concerned it wouldn't matter, 'you can make a start on the house. You'll find plenty there to keep you occupied.'

'I wouldn't want to change it too much,' she answered dubiously. 'I like it as it is. When we were married I thought it looked beautiful.'

'For the,' he didn't say 'our', 'wedding, flowers covered a multitude of sins, but there won't be any flowers today.'

Eden shivered, trying not to believe there was a hidden warning in his voice. 'Can you afford it?' she asked uncertainly.

'We might do a little at a time,' he allowed. 'Perhaps make a start on the rooms downstairs.'

'Will we be doing much entertaining?' she glanced at him anxiously, thinking she might have a lot to learn.

'Not immediately,' he glanced impatiently at his wristwatch. 'I haven't decided about accepting any invitations yet, either.'

'To save money?'

'Partly.' His face and eyes lightened with relief as he saw the truck coming. 'We may as well cash in somehow on our unhappy circumstances. People accept that a newly married couple can find their own entertainment.'

Eden was still smarting from his harsh sarcasm when they reached the plantation. Vern, fortunately, was too busy talking with the driver to notice how pale she had gone. The sight of the old Colonial-style house acted like a balm on her sore heart, and she felt much more herself by the time they were inside. Here, they discovered that both Jessie and Faith were out having tea with a neighbour.

Eden knew a twinge of guilt for feeling glad that Jessie wasn't there to welcome them. She needed an hour or two to settle in without the added tension of Jessie's snide remarks and hostile stares.

Mrs Prince beamed on them, her growing affection for Mr Vern's young wife very apparent as she asked if they had enjoyed their trip and offered tea.

Vern said, yes, they had had a good trip, and refused tea. 'I want a word with Willis, but my wife might like some?'

Startled, Eden glanced at him, a pulse jerking uncomfortably in her throat. He called her his wife, but she wondered if he meant her to realise that, in her case, it was a completely empty title. She could almost hear him mentally adding, 'The honeymoon's over!'

As she became aware of Mrs Prince looking at her enquiringly, she nodded gratefully before asking quickly, 'I expect my father's all right, Mrs Prince?'

'We've only been gone a week, Eden, for Pete's sake!' Vern exclaimed tersely, whipping her right out from under the housekeeper's nose and dragging her upstairs. 'I'll show you your room.'

'What will Mrs Prince think?' Eden retorted resentfully, trying unsuccessfully to free her arm from the grip of steely fingers. Yet she did feel happier when he referred to her room, since it seemed to indicate that she was going to be allowed some privacy.

At the top of the stairs he let go of her and she followed him with a slightly lighter heart. When her room, however, turned out to be his room, she hesitated nervously in the doorway.

'There's only one bed.' Her eyes widened uncertainly. 'Why have you stopped here?'

'Because this is where you're to sleep!' He swung

back to her, staring straight at her, so she couldn't misunderstand. 'With me.'

'No!' she cried.

'Yes!' he said, picking her up, disregarding her angry surprise as he carried her over the threshold. Unkindly he asked, as he dumped her on the bed, 'Do you require a further demonstration?'

Winded, from the way in which he almost threw her down, Eden gazed up at him, fighting for breath. 'I—I didn't think you'd want me anywhere near you.'

'I don't, not particularly,' he replied, killing the small ray of hope in Eden's eyes almost before it was born, 'but, apart from appearances—to which civilised man has become pathetically addicted, I want you where I can keep an eye on you. I won't have you slipping out in the middle of the night.'

Utterly bewildered, she asked, 'Where would I go?'

'Who knows?' he shrugged, boredom creeping into his voice as he began unbuttoning his shirt.

'What are you doing?' she whispered, her eyes riveted, almost in shock on the widening expanse of hair-covered chest.

'Not giving Mrs Prince more food for thought than she already has,' he mocked softly, 'by going to bed with you.'

'You wouldn't?' she choked unevenly, her senses suddenly swimming as she heard his breathing change, becoming fast and rough.

'If things had been different,' he retorted savagely, 'you might have been lucky to get down for dinner!' Abruptly, after one more mocking and fully comprehensive glance, he left her, disappearing into his dressing-room and emerging several minutes later, dressed to go out.

'I'll see you later,' he said, harsh amusement in his eyes as he saw how, in his absence, Eden had scrambled hastily off the bed and was sitting by the dressing-table, vigorously brushing her long, shining hair.

Eden shivered as he went out, trying futilely to stop her pulses racing. Vern's expression had clearly indicated that not for one moment did he believe the energy she was putting into what she was doing was responsible for her hectically flushed cheeks. If he had taken her in his arms, there on the bed, she knew she mightn't have been able to resist him, and she was becoming more afraid of herself than of him. While she was fully aware that she loved him, she hadn't been prepared for so powerful an emotion and it threatened to take her over completely.

If things had been different, she thought unhappily, laying down her hairbrush and slowly following him downstairs, he might have waited and had tea with her. She hadn't been paying much attention to what the man with the truck had been saying to him as they had driven from the coast, but she didn't think it could have been anything urgent enough to justify Vern leaving the house in such a hurry.

She was glad he wasn't there though, when, an hour later Faith and Jessie returned.

'We left early,' Faith explained, after kissing Eden warmly. 'Jessie didn't feel well.'

If Jessie wasn't feeling well, it didn't affect the sharpness of her tongue. When Faith excused herself to rest and change before dinner, Jessie lost no time in declaring that she had no intention of relinquishing her position as mistress of the house.

'As long as I'm here the servants will take orders from me,' she said coldly. 'I've already told them.'

Eden swallowed and said doggedly, 'Vern might expect me to give the orders.'

'Then you can tell him you don't want the responsibility,' Jessie replied tartly.

'Perhaps I do.' Eden tried to speak firmly, but

wondered despairingly what happiness there would be for any of them if Jessie continued with this atittude. At a guess, the house practically ran itself and she couldn't imagine Mrs Prince taking kindly to anyone throwing their weight about. As she was Vern's wife, Mrs Prince would naturally expect to consult her over various things, but Eden didn't think she would be prepared to accept two mistresses.

'I won't argue with you,' Jessie exclaimed, glaring at her, 'but just try and assert yourself over me and you'll soon discover whose side Vern is on!'

Eden was asleep when Vern came to bed that night and in the morning he was gone before she woke up. With nerves as tense as they had been during dinner, she had lain awake in the huge bed, waiting for him to come up. When he hadn't appeared after midnight she must have fallen asleep. Dinner had proved a difficult meal, with Vern clearly abstracted for most of the time and failing to notice the venomous little glances Jessie was forever shooting at his wife. Eden had never felt so uncomfortable in her life.

When Jessie had announced that she had invited the Darels, brother and sister, to dinner the following evening, Vern had frowned, but he hadn't actually said anything. Eden hadn't known what to make of it until Jessie had added that they might be staying for a few days again. Then, when he suddenly smiled, she had realised how much he was obviously looking forward to seeing Carita, and her spirits had dropped.

It was early, but finding herself full of a kind of restless energy, Eden decided to get up. After a quick shower, she put on a cool cotton shirt and matching top in a flattering pale green and after giving her hair a quick brush she ran downstairs. If the Darels were coming it wouldn't be practical to begin at once on the house, so if Vern didn't mind she might go and see Joe.

She was surprised to find him at breakfast, having

expected she might have to hunt all over the estate for him. He was wearing a pair of light pants and an open-necked shirt and looked so handsome and virile that her limbs felt weak and trembling.

'You look a bit shaken. Hadn't you better sit down?' he got to his feet and came round the table to pull a chair out for her. Before she took it she made the mistake of turning her head to meet his hard, bright stare and drew a sharp breath as she suddenly saw his pupils dilate. She tried to look away, but couldn't, and her pulse began to quicken in dizzying reaction.

In a second he had released the chair and was dragging her against him, his mouth searching for her own. Eden was too dazed to try and avoid him. She felt the race of her heart increase so rapidly as her lips parted under his fierce kiss that she thought she might faint.

Trembling, she slid her hands up his chest to clasp his neck, feeling the tension in the rigid muscles under her palms. His hair was thick and crisp, and she buried her fingers in it, feeling them tingle. As he went on kissing her passionately, her whole body became alive with a kind of pleading, fevered response which had her melting against him helplessly.

He moved back, breathing jerkily. She felt him staring at her. 'You were asleep when I came to bed, last night,' he said thickly. 'No wonder I feel tired! I watched you for hours, but you never flickered an eyelid.'

She did now. Her lids felt heavy, but she forced herself to raise them, to look at him. Was he trying to tell her he had wanted her, or was he just tormenting her?

His mouth had a drowsy movement to it which aroused a dangerous excitement inside her. 'Would you like to go back to bed?' he muttered, eyes darkening.

There was a rattle of coffee pots in the hall and Mrs

Prince came in, not at all embarrassed to find them drawing apart with some reluctance. Eden sat down quickly, colour mounting in her cheeks as she tried to steady her voice enough to say, 'Good morning.'

When Mrs Prince had gone, Vern didn't attempt to take her in his arms again. He returned to his own chair with a coolness that made Eden wonder just what kind of game he was playing with her.

After pouring two cups of coffee, he passed her one, his eyes lingering mockingly on her flawless complexion. 'In the nick of time, wouldn't you say?'

Eden, struggling to pull herself together, found that didn't help. She had no wish to contemplate Vern carrying her upstairs, locking the bedroom door and slowly undressing her. Hoping her voice sounded cooler than she felt, she ignored his remark and said she was thinking of going to see her father. She had been going to ask if he would mind, but she suddenly decided not to.

Vern didn't object. He didn't even seem interested. His dark eyes were still on her but he seemed to be thinking of other things. 'When do you want to go?'

'Oh,' such an easy victory took her by surprise, 'I—well, after lunch, I thought. This morning I wondered if Jessie would like a dip in the pool. If I could persuade her I'm sure it would do her good.'

'As long as you don't go about it like a bull in a china shop,' Vern replied curtly. 'She's a very sensitive girl.'

'I do have some sense!' Eden retorted, but later she wondered if that was true.

Jessie did allow Eden to coax her to sunbathe and said she might, if she felt like it, try the pool. Having kept Eden running all morning, ordering her around like a servant, Jessie was now stretched out on a lounger by the pool, enjoying the sun. At least, Eden hoped she was. It had been quite a mammoth task getting Jessie even this far. Persuading her to change into a bikini had proved exhausting.

Eden glanced down at her as she lay with her eyes closed. Jessie had an extremely shapely figure, if only she could be convinced she wasn't maimed for life and didn't have to hide it! Eden frowned, uncertain as to what to do next. She was having to work purely by instinct. Apart from Joe and his desire to retreat from the world, she had had no experience of this kind of thing before. Should she insist that Jessie joined her in the water immediately, or wait until she had had a rest?

Eventually Eden decided that if Jessie saw her swimming she might not be able to resist coming in, and this might be the wisest form of persuasion.

She swam several lengths of the pool before climbing out again when, to her delight, she noticed Jessie leave her lounger and wander to the edge. 'Coming in?' she smiled, and it wasn't easy to smile in the face of Jessie's sullen expression.

Jessie had an odd look about her. Brushing her streaming hair aside, Eden stared at her closely, feeling puzzled. She felt even more puzzled when Jessie suddenly stumbled sideways and fell, with a shriek and a clumsy splash, on her back into the water. When Vern unexpectedly rounded the corner, Eden shot him a frantic glance before diving in after her.

Jessie was choking and spluttering, clearly in need of help, which Eden tried to give by putting an arm round her.

With a wild sob, Jessie shook it off, glaring at her furiously before turning to her brother. 'Didn't you see her push me in?'

Vern hushed her, lifting her gently out while she clung to him frantically. 'Why should she, Jessie?'

Jessie's voice rose hysterically. 'Perhaps because Martin's coming tonight and she'd like to see me in bed so she can have him all to herself. She's been asking enough questions about him!'

Immediately Vern's mouth tightened. Reaching for a towel, he draped it over his seemingly trembling sister. 'You mustn't alarm yourself, Jessie. I'll be here to see nothing like that happens.'

Over Jessie's head, his eyes met Eden's and she shrank from the anger in them. He was silently accusing her of hating Jessie, and for a moment Eden might almost have agreed with him. But if she hated Jessie it was for what Jessie had done to her, not the other way round. It would be no good attempting to defend herself, though, for, as usual, Jessie had made sure she had no evidence to support her, should she try.

'I'll go and get dressed,' she said hollowly, almost able to see the blaze of victory on Jessie's face as Vern led her carefully away.

After lunch, from which Jessie was absent, Eden left to visit Joe. Vern, who had scarcely spoken to her throughout the meal, said he would get someone to take her and they could wait and bring her back.

Eden didn't want the driver waiting. She wanted to spend the whole afternoon at her old home to try and relax. The situation here seemed to be threatening her sanity and she knew she had to get away by herself for a while.

As she hesitated, wondering illogically how to explain this without putting it in words, Faith apparently thought she knew what was worrying her. 'The Darels are coming, but not until this evening, dear, and that's all been taken care of. Jessie has seen to everything.'

Faith meant well, Eden could tell. She might love her niece, but she wasn't blind to Jessie's faults as Vern was. She even occasionally took Eden's side when Jessie spoke sharply to her, when Vern wasn't there. She couldn't know that this time she wasn't helping Eden at all.

Vern said frostily, as Eden had feared he might, 'Isn't it about time you took over? As my wife you have certain responsibilities.'

Eden nodded uneasily and hurried out, unwilling to enter into another futile argument. No doubt Vern wouldn't let the matter rest there. His fury had been smouldering, she guessed, for all his outward icy appearance, ever since Jessie had fallen in the pool, but while in the privacy of their bedroom she might be willing to endure his harsh castigations, she certainly wasn't going to with Faith looking on!

Vern had no idea what he was talking about when he accused her of avoiding her responsibilities, but, she conceded, he might be justified in a way. After breakfast, Eden had decided to see Mrs Prince about this evening's dinner and accommodation for the Darels, only to find that Jessie had beaten her to it.

'Miss Jessie and I have it all arranged, dear,' Mrs Prince smiled happily. 'I quite understand you wanting her to carry on as she's been doing, until you get used to the house, and a few more weeks aren't going to make any difference. It might even do Miss Jessie good, I'm thinking.'

Because she wondered if this might be right, Eden had merely nodded and not bothered to dispute Jessie's fictitious allegations. Sometimes she was given to thinking that Jessie couldn't be all bad, the way she had everyone, including herself, giving her such consideration. Now she would have to think up a suitable excuse when Vern tackled her over the housekeeping later, and she felt suddenly very weary.

Joe was delighted to see her and to her astonishment she found him surprisingly active. He looked younger, his expression more alert, his clothes, which he had been wont to throw on and off like rags, neater. Eden had to remind herself, as Vern had said, that she had only been gone a week!

'I don't know how it happened,' Joe confessed, with a little of her own uncertainty when she felt forced to ask him. 'The whole business of the house and land, then you getting married, seems to have given me the jolt I must have needed.'

The house was spick-and-span, he had even begun painting again.

'Nothing much,' he grinned sheepishly. 'Of course I've only just got started. A seascape? Yes. I'm not sure yet whether it's going to be any good or not, though.'

Eden knew. He allowed her a glimpse of it and it showed remarkable promise. 'Oh, Dad,' she exclaimed, hugging him, 'I can't believe it!'

He laughed with an anticipatory glint in his eye she had never thought to see again. Then he sobered, glancing at her sharply, as if suddenly noticing she was paler and thinner.

'How was the honeymoon?' he asked abruptly.

Eden was thankful that it didn't take long to convince him that the honeymoon had been wonderful.

'Jessie, then?' he frowned, making her realise he suspected something was badly wrong.

'Oh, she has her good days and her bad ones,' Eden replied evasively, pretending to believe he was merely asking after Jessie's health.

'So I gathered,' he said dryly, shooting Eden another sharp glance. 'At a guess I'd say that girl was more in need of a psychiatrist than anything else.'

'I'm sure she'll be fine, Dad. Stop worrying!'

'I'm not worrying,' he retorted unconvincingly. 'Well,' he admitted reluctantly, 'I suppose I am in a way. Someone like that can have a very bruising effect, but as long as Vern's around I know she won't be allowed to get at you.'

Blankly for a moment, Eden stared at him, then turned her head. If only he knew!

CHAPTER NINE

EDEN, disregarding Vern's orders, had told the driver to return to the plantation and come back for her at five, and she was rather startled when Vern came for her himself. She wondered why he had. He must intend making sure she didn't stay too long.

After talking to Joe for a while, he said they must leave as they were expecting guests.

Joe said to him, not too seriously, as he came to see them off, 'Eden looks a bit peaky. You aren't beating her already, by any chance?'

'Sometimes I'm tempted to,' Vern replied in the same vein, making Joe laugh.

'Been complaining, have you?' Vern snapped shortly, as they drove away.

Eden asked, a bitter smile on her face, 'What have I to complain of?'

'That's one question I can easily answer. Nothing!'

Sadly Eden wondered where the rapport they had shared earlier in the day had gone. Killed by Jessie's scheming and Joe's well-meant intervention, she supposed, to say nothing of Vern's determination to think the worst of her!

'What time will our guests be arriving?' She adopted a deliberately couldn't-care-less attitude because the hurt in her cried out to annoy him.

That she had succeeded was clear by the way his jaw hardened as he shot furiously over the main road. 'You told me you weren't interested in other men.'

'I'm not . . .' She had been flung against the door and, as she straightened, she wondered what was coming next. Not an apology, that was for sure! She

150

didn't like the dark red colour in his face.

'You didn't deny it when Jessie said you'd been asking questions about Martin Darel.'

'I can't deny it,' she confessed, biting her lip, 'but it wasn't what you think. I was trying to arouse Jessie's interest, not express my own. You mentioned that she liked him and I thought it might help.'

'Hmm . . .'

She glanced at his strong profile, seeing a shadow of uncertainty on it. Impulsively she added, 'I didn't push Jessie into the pool, you know. She might think I did, but I didn't touch her.'

He shrugged, and while he didn't actually admit that Jessie could have made a mistake, he obviously wasn't prepared to argue over it.

When he didn't speak, Eden allowed her eyes to linger on the breadth of his broad shoulders. His shirt was soaked in sweat and clinging to him, revealing the hard sinew and muscle underneath. She laced her fingers together to try and stop them shaking while she diverted her too wayward thoughts elsewhere.

He must have been working hard since lunch. Her growing interest in the plantation removed a little of the torment from Eden's heart. She had lived near it all her life but never had a proper look around it.

'I noticed some trucks bringing cattle, earlier,' she said haltingly.

'I'm going to raise more beef and sugar,' he replied briefly.

She tried again. 'Will you be keeping George Willis on, now that you're going to be here all the time yourself?'

'For the time being.' He slapped an insect off one of his powerful arms. 'There's a lot to do, a lot of catching up to do, perhaps I should say, and I need someone to take over when I have to be away. As it happens, Willis is nearing retirement age and wants to be relieved of the overall responsibility, which suits me fine.'

Eden lapsed into silence as the house came in view. It was probably just as well that Vern was going to be busy, if she was, too, over the next few weeks, mightn't the problem of Jessie resolve itself and the tension ease?

The Darels arrived while they were changing for dinner. They were late, it appeared later because of being held up, but Vern swiftly finished dressing and went to welcome them, leaving Eden to follow more leisurely. Deliberately she took advantage of his absence and chose an elegant white dress, one of her trousseau ones, as yet unworn. She was rather uncertain about the cobwebby top, but it did things for her, she reflected, studying herself in the mirror after putting it on. The cut of it was deceptively simple and its colour lent a very bridal look while it suggested something far from innocent. Eden felt her cheeks colour faintly, while she didn't try and discover what it was for herself. She had to try and compete with Miss Darel's elegance, hadn't she? With her brown hair floating in a silky, perfumed cloud about her small, beautiful head, her face discretely made up with the merest gloss of pink lipstick outlining her soft, full mouth, she almost felt she might be able to do so.

The sudden silence which greeted her as she opened the drawing-room door convinced her that she had made an impression, though what sort she wasn't sure. She feared she had made another mistake when she saw Martin's eyes widen with admiration, but Vern appeared cleverly to be ready to deal with any hopes he might be entertaining. In two strides, with an audibly drawn breath which Eden hoped no one else heard, he was by her side, pulling her close, kissing her lightly on the lips.

'You'll have to excuse us,' he drawled with deceiving humour, 'but we're just newly married. The novelty of being a husband hasn't yet worn off.' Under cover of laughter, edged with varying degrees of amusement, he snarled in undertones at Eden, 'Couldn't you find something that left more to the imagination?'

Aware as she was of Jessie's and Carita's antagonism and Vern's disapproving eyes, despite George Willis's friendly overtures, the evening took a lot of getting through. Vern might denounce her for looking at other men, but he didn't seem to think there was anything wrong with other women looking at him. Indeed, it frequently seemed to Eden that he was responding with an indecent lack of unwillingnes to Carita's glowing glances and fawning hands.

Jessie, having apparently recovered from her ordeal in the pool, monopolised Martin's attention. Eden suddenly realised that though they might not know it yet themselves, they were deeply attracted to each other. If their friendship progressed would Jessie tell him about Diego Dexter? Martin might be easygoing, but Eden sensed he had his share of pride when it came to the serious things in life. Few men, today, expected to marry a virgin, but he might not be prepared to tolerate the alarming tangle of Jessie's deceitful lies. If Martin proposed and Jessie agreed to marry him, any hope of her confessing anything, even to Vern, would be doomed. She would never risk it! Sadly, Eden felt the flicker of new optimism she had known a few hours ago slowly fade.

She had expected Vern to be late in coming to bed, but he followed her almost immediately. Her heart hammered against her ribs as he closed their door and locked it. The key turning had a curious sound nothing to do with the actual operation. It was the first time he had locked it since they had returned from their honeymoon.

Going to stand by the dressing-table, she waited for him to go through to his dressing-room before she began taking her clothes off. When he merely sat down on the edge of the bed, without any obvious intention of going farther, she looked at him in surprise.

'Carry on,' he shrugged, 'don't mind me. And don't pretend you're shy.'

'I was about to take a shower,' she stammered hastily, avoiding his eyes. 'I—I was surprised to see you so soon, that's all.'

'It's after midnight,' he said blandly. 'And I didn't accuse you of being surprised.'

'I only thought . . .'

'Well, don't,' he interrupted curtly. 'Go and have your shower. I'll have one after you.'

She recognised he was in a peculiar mood, although she might be hard put to define it. With fumbling hands she gathered up her night clothes, departing fully dressed. She was shy, but she wasn't telling him that! 'I won't be long,' she said.

A spacious cupboard in the bathroom provided a temporary home for her white gown while she flung her nightdress carelessly over the bath. As the water sprayed over her head, over the top of her cap, she debated what Vern was trying to do. Make her nervous, perhaps? As he hadn't made love to her since their second night on the boat, she didn't think he would bother now, especially after the languishing glances Carita had been bestowing on him all evening! Jealousy of the other girl flared, an emotion so new to Eden that she wasn't immediately able to control it. How was she to live through the long days of Carita's visit, when she and Vern appeared to find so much pleasure in each other's company?

Tears washed down Eden's cheeks with the water, and the first she knew of Vern's presence was when the shower door was pulled open and he was in beside her. The first words of protest hadn't passed her lips before his own were on them, silencing her. His mouth, hard and possessive, was on hers, crushing the breath out of her before she could even take a gulp of the air she needed.

Eden had never known anything like it—yet, she asked herself, didn't she experience this feeling every time he kissed her? She could feel the racing beat of his heart, his strong bare limbs against her while his hands explored and his mouth bruised.

Water ran over them, cooling their skin while the fires raging inside them diminished any feeling of relief. She could feel the heat from Vern's body burning her up, absorbing her like a furnace, intent on devouring her completely. Passion incited their senses, demolishing all sensible thought. The shock Eden had fleetingly felt at such an invasion of her privacy faded. She lay against him conscious only of the deep beating of his heart as his kisses demanded her total surrender.

Holding her from him, he turned off the shower. Slowly her dazed eyes opened to wander over him, taking in the different textures of his hair-roughened skin.

'You look about seventeen,' he said thickly, pulling off her shower cap.

'Why are you here?' she whispered.

'The million dollar question,' his voice was sardonic while the green eyes leapt darkly. 'Do I really have to answer it?'

She tried to think. 'I didn't expect . . .'

'Isn't it better than a lot of preliminiary skirmishing?' he cut in harshly, 'with people saying things they don't mean?'

'You really believe that?'

For a moment his mouth tightened. 'Women have to hear that a man adores them, even when they know it's far from the truth.'

'It would take a long time to convince me,' she said unevenly.

'More than I have to spare, I think,' he grated, as she began to struggle, forcing him to hold her closer, clearly arousing him again. 'Let's get out of here,' she heard him exclaim.

'We're both wet!'

'We'll soon dry.' He picked her up, carrying her back to the bedroom and laying her on the bed. He came down beside her as she weakly tried to avoid him. With a smothered groan he muttered against her mutinous lips, 'In another moment you won't care.'

She tried to fight him, but as his mouth teased and his hands caressed, all her resistance faded. While his mouth explored hers sensuously, his hands cupped her breasts, arousing her to ecstasy before sliding to other vulnerable places. Every bit of her body seemed to be dissolving in the heat generating between them and she was helpless in the grip of her ever-increasing desire for him.

Afterwards she was to recall what he had said about preliminary skirmishing with some bewilderment. Embarrassment, too, when she remembered how, in the end, her own fevered impatience might have been even greater than his. Soon he had her clinging to him, almost begging for release, half frantic that although he didn't try and hide how much he wanted her, he didn't hurry.

Breathing thickly, he kissed her deeply, and because she was young, her body capable of endless loving, Eden didn't want to hold back. When at last Vern took her she was receptive to such a degree that his control splintered savagely, and the subsequent culmination stunned them both.

The Darels stayed two days. Eden had suspected that Jessie might have asked them solely from a desire to hurt her, but she swiftly came to the conclusion that she might be wrong. She became convinced that Jessie was falling in love, and, Eden thought bitterly, she should know the signs, for wasn't she in love herself? Unfortunately, in her case, with a man who didn't love her.

During the two days of the Darels' visit, Vern took them all out. Faith only came with them on the second evening, when they went out to dinner. She said she had seen most of the island and, at her age, she found the daytime heat a little trying. Eden would have liked to have stayed at home as well, but Vern wouldn't allow it, and although she resented his high-handedness, she had to admit that she enjoyed seeing more of Jamaica than she had done so far. The Darels readily confessed that although they spent a lot of time in Jamaica they had certainly not seen all of it, and Eden concluded that the care Vern took in organising their schedule was for their benefit rather than hers.

Perhaps Eden enjoyed most her trip up the Martha Brae, one of Jamaica's rafting rivers, but she wasn't sure if that was because Carita refused to go, and, as Martin offered to stay with her, Jessie wouldn't go either. Eden and Vern started from Rafters' Village, where they left the others having refreshments, and drifted for an hour on specially constructed bamboo rafts through banana plantations, fields of yam and sugarcane. They finished at Rock, where Vern had arranged for Martin to meet them.

From there they went on to Falmouth, the capital of the parish of Trelawny. It was named after the Falmouth in Cornwall, the birthplace of Governor William Trelawny. Vern pointed out the Methodist manse, at the bottom of Market Street, built in 1799 by the Barretts, the family of the poet, Elizabeth Barrett Browning. They also visited Greenwood House, one of the great estates in the area, dating from the early nineteenth century, which used to be owned by the Barretts. And Rose Hall, reputed to have once been the home of an infamous white witch who murdered her husbands. It had been restored at great expense and was thought to be one of the finest houses on the island, with its mahogany panelling, precious fruitwood and magnificent staircase.

They went home that day around the top of the north coast, taking in Negril, Jamaica's latest tourist development, as Carita expressed great interest in it. There was a seven-mile stretch of wonderful beach and while none of its beauty appeared to have been destroyed, Eden noticed Vern's mouth tighten and guessed he was thinking that no place was invulnerable. It made her feel glad suddenly, despite her heartache, that he was now guardian of their own little stretch. At least he would try and make sure nothing like this happened to it.

After the Darels left, Jessie was morose and given to long silences. She seemed like someone with a lot on their mind, and Eden concluded that she was thinking of Martin. Yet her overall demeanour puzzled Eden. She had thought Jessie was falling in love, but now she found herself doubting it. Each day seemed to find her more vicious than ever. Constantly she made scenes without provocation and appeared determined to make Eden's life a complete misery.

She appeared to have forgotten all about running the house, however, and the responsibility for this now fell on Eden's shoulders. While Eden was gratified at how easily she slipped into this new role, the strain of everything was telling. She grew pale and thinner and was sleeping badly.

During the day, she spent a lot of time avoiding Vern, but at night it wasn't so easy, and he didn't allow her much sleep. Since the night he had carried her from the shower, he seemed to have forgotten the former control he had put on himself. He made love to her continually, sometimes almost violently, although always silently. It was his silence which Eden was coming to dread most. While she couldn't prevent herself from responding to him, with a wantonness she felt often ashamed of, she yearned for him to speak to her tenderly.

He did speak to her one evening after making love to her, but it wasn't tenderly. As he rolled over to his own side of the bed, he muttered harshly, 'We should have had a longer honeymoon, then we wouldn't have been suffering from this kind of hangover.'

Eden, when she was able to say anything, forbore to remind him that he had scarcely touched her during their honeymoon, nor appeared to want to! It seemed to Eden that he sometimes despised himself for his apparently increasing desire for her, and she tried not to object to what she miserably thought of as being used. Anything was better than being without him, and physically they were perfectly matched, but it was his love that her whole being cried out for.

With the help of an extremely clever and capable decorator, from a firm Faith had recommended, Eden had almost finalised her plans for the downstairs rooms. At this stage Jessie decided to go and visit the Darels. She refused to stay at the plantation while the house was being pulled to pieces, she said. Eden suspected her real reason for going was that Martin had asked her so frequently. He was always on the phone, and Eden wondered why Jessie had hesitated so long when she was clearly eager to go.

Vern, having a business appointment in Kingston the following day, arranged to take her. He asked Eden to accompany them, and though she didn't want to, she couldn't think of a good enough excuse. The actual work on the decorating wasn't due to start for a few days yet and Mrs Prince was more than able to manage on her own.

'I shan't be there long,' said Vern, finding her in their

bedroom after breakfast, on the morning of Jessie's departure, 'and a day out might do you good.'

'Do I look in need of one?' she asked sharply.

He shot her a quick glance but only said, 'Get ready. We'll be leaving within the hour.'

'What if I don't want to come?'

'Shut up, there's a good girl,' he smiled, going through to his dressing-room to find a fresh shirt, which he changed in front of her. 'Why don't you just do as you're told?'

When Vern smiled like that it meant she had no choice but to do as he asked. She had seen him use the very same smile and tone before—there was little humour in it. It wasn't reserved for her alone, but she knew its power. He was very much the boss of his domain and made sure everyone was aware of it. Even George Willis didn't hesitate to do his bidding. Vern wasn't used to being opposed, especially by his wife.

'Will you be staying at the Darels' house long?' she hedged, feeling unable to face seeing him with Carita.

'No,' swiftly he knotted a tie around his strong throat, 'only long enough to drop Jessie off, I promise you. I want to get my business over in good time. On the way home we might stop off somewhere for dinner.'

The Darels lived in an uptown house, in the cooler foothills of the Blue Mountains. Jessie, looking strangely animated, waved them goodbye, and for once Vern made no curt remark about her condition. Eden had managed to persuade Jessie to try the pool again and lately she had spent many hours there. Vern had been adamant that Eden kept a close watch over her, despite the abundance of domestic staff, and she had been hard pushed to fit this in along with her sessions with Mrs Prince and the decorators.

Jessie looked well from it, though. Today she was wearing a pair of white cotton slacks, but, without them, her legs had tanned to a golden brown, and, as Eden had predicted, her scars were scarcely noticeable.

Because Eden had no desire to go shopping or sightseeing on her own, Vern took her to the offices of the firm he was visiting with him. She was surprised to notice how well the staff in the large office block appeared to know him. He asked her to wait and, as a smiling secretary brought her coffee, Eden glanced around curiously, being quite unfamiliar with surroundings like these, either in the capital or elsewhere. It appeared to have something to do with the bauxite alumina industry. On their way out, when Vern returned, she asked him, but he was extremely reticent. He did admit, however, that he had shares in the company and was, in fact, one of its directors.

This information startled Eden as she realised it might explain his mysterious visits to Kingston? And while she wasn't foolish enough to dismiss Carita's attraction altogether, it somehow made her feel better.

They did have dinner on their way home and surprisingly he was very pleasant to her. Eden wondered sadly if he was beginning to forgive her for Jessie but she couldn't decide. She only knew it was heaven to bask in the warmth of his friendlier manner and she wished it could last for ever. It did last throughout the entire evening and even when they got home, in the privacy of their bedroom, although he kissed her passionately, he was very gentle with her.

The following day he was busy, but his good mood continued. It wasn't until the next morning that Eden noticed a change, if not enough to alarm her, to begin with.

She had almost finished dressing to go down for breakfast when he came in. He hadn't disturbed her when he had got up, she guessed hours ago, and she had overslept. She thought this was what was wrong when he glanced at her coldly, though he didn't usually complain when he found her in bed.

'I won't be a minute,' she assured him hurriedly, but when he didn't reply she asked uncertainly if there was anything wrong.

He glanced at her narrowly, his green eyes still cool on her suddenly anxious face. 'Do you remember the earrings I once gave you, Eden? You said you'd sold them.'

Because she had lied to him, she flushed, She managed a jerky nod while feeling terribly guilty. If he asked whom she had sold them to she didn't know what she was going to say.

She heard his voice, an icy drawl, shattering the fragile, newly established warmth between them. 'I wonder if you'll ever learn to tell me the truth, Eden?'

'What do you mean?' she whispered, her face white.

He didn't beat about the bush. On a harsh breath, he said. 'I took my cuff-links out here last night, you may or may not remember? This morning when I noticed them on your dressing-table and went to pick them up, one of them fell into your drawer, which was slightly open. Naturally, to recover it, I had to open the drawer wider. It was then that I saw the earrings, the ones I'd given you on your eighteenth birthday.'

Eden wished the floor might have opened and swallowed her up! Last night she had been looking at the earrings, wishing she could wear them. She had been wondering, as she often did, if she could tell him about them, but before she could make up her mind she had heard him coming to dress for dinner. Hastily she had dropped them in the drawer nearest to her, rather than the usual place where she kept them. She had intended doing that later, but Vern had come up to bed with her and she had had no chance. It wasn't their value, or even the sentiment attached to the earrings, she suspected, that was making Vern so angry. It was because he believed she had deliberately tried to deceive him.

The harmony between them had been too good to

last. Bitterly she thought she might have known something would happen to shatter it. But this time she could only blame herself. How could she confess that she had used the earrings impulsively, as the only weapon she had?

Staring at Vern's hard face, she knew it wouldn't be easy, but she did attempt to be honest. 'I pretended I'd sold them to—to try and hurt you, because . . .'

Furiously he cut in, 'Don't you think you've hurt me enough?'

'You can't blame me for the land!' Eden's voice trembled desperately. 'I realise you had to have it, but it wasn't my fault you hadn't enough to pay for it outright. At least,' she stumbled on, her words, like her thoughts becoming more disjointed, 'I can't be any worse than the girl, Rona, in the States who refused to marry you because you were poor . . .'

His eyes sharpened. 'Who told you about her?'

Eden suddenly realising she had betrayed Jessie's confidence, stammered unhappily, 'I forget.'

'Okay,' he snapped curtly. 'It's of no consequence anyway. What's more important is your dishonesty. It corrodes everything. I think we need time apart.'

'T-time apart?' Her face went even paler.

'I don't mean parted,' he rasped. 'I'll be out for most of the day and this evening I shan't be in for dinner. And, from now on, I'll sleep in my dressing-room.'

Eden sat down abruptly, her head bowed, her chest tight with sheer, aching misery. 'If that's what you want . . .?'

'It is.' His cold glance cut through her, then turning abruptly, as though the sight of her pained him, he muttered something under his breath and went out.

The morning dragged so much, even with Faith for company, that after lunch, when Faith went for her usual rest, Eden told her that she had decided to go and see Joe.

'I haven't seen him for almost a week,' she said.

Faith smiled understandingly. 'You must miss him, dear. Get one of the men to drive you. Ring George Willis.'

'No, it doesn't matter.' She knew he would be busy when Vern wasn't here. Vern had gone to Kingston. He hadn't told her, Faith had. Eden hadn't seen him since he had left their room, but Faith appeared to imagine it had been her idea that he should go and see Jessie. Whether Vern had implied this, or Faith merely took it for granted, Eden didn't try and discover. She guessed unhappily that Vern had really gone to Kingston to see Carita. She hadn't missed the open invitation in the glance Carita had bestowed on him on the day they had dropped Jessie off. 'The walk will do me good,' she smiled, the effort making her realise how stiff her facial muscles had become.

'Take care,' Faith said anxiously.

A long walk, even in the heat of the day, didn't normally tire Eden and she was surprised to find herself exhausted long before she reached her old home. She wondered if she had been working too hard lately or if it was because of this latest rift between herself and Vern. A great weight seemed to be lying on her, making her feel almost ill.

She found her father in his studio working. 'Hello, Dad,' she said, putting her head round the door.

He glanced over his shoulder absently but with something like relief in his eyes when he saw who it was. 'Oh, it's only you!'

'What a welcome!' she said wryly.

'Oh, you know how it is,' he shrugged, laying down his brushes before turning to take another, closer look at her. 'There's nothing wrong, is there?'

'No, nothing,' she lied, thinking she was getting good at it. Wandering further into the room, she tried to get a better view of what he was doing. 'Can't I come to see my own father without an inquisition?'

His eyes narrowed at her tone and he frowned.

'I'm sorry, Dad,' she forced a remorseful smile, 'I didn't mean to snap, and you're quite right—I was in a black mood. I came out to get rid of it.'

'Not on me, I hope? Where's Vern?'

'Away for the day.'

'Ah, that explains it!' Joe relaxed. 'He'll come back.'

She didn't argue. It was better that he should believe she was merely missing her husband and indulging in a little feminine perversity. When he read her a gentle lecture about the foolishness of being too possessive, she endured it silently.

'Look, Dad,' she said, as he paused, 'I can see you're busy. I think I'll find a can of lemonade and have a wander on the beach. Then, if you can spare the time later, perhaps we could have tea together?'

'Fine,' he grinned. 'I would like to get this finished. Why not have coffee, though? I could do with a cup.'

After taking him a mug of coffee, she sat and drank her own on the porch. Surprisingly she felt better and realised Joe must have guessed she was in need of something, even if he hadn't let on.

Feeling grateful for his astuteness which he often concealed far too well, she decided to find her old bikini and go for a swim. The sea, with the waves breaking lazily on the white shore, looked very inviting. It was one of the few things Eden missed on the plantation, having the sea on her doorstep.

She walked to the end of the beach, to her favourite spot just out of sight of the house before she went in. The water was just right and she found it so relaxing that she swam for an hour before coming out again. With her hair streaming over her eyes, she thought the man coming from the trees towards her was Vern. Her heart sank, because he had warned her about swimming alone and she didn't know if she could face his fury twice in the same day. Then her sense of shock increased as she brushed the water from her eyes and saw that it wasn't Vern but Diego Dexter. As her horrified gaze swept over him, he halted in front of her.

'Hello, Eden,' he smiled. 'I've waited a long time to catch you.'

'Mr Dexter!' she exclaimed, all the colour leaving her face.

'Come on,' he jeered, 'why don't you ask?'

'Ask—what?' she gasped blankly.

'What are you doing here? The standard question.'

'What are you?' she whispered hoarsely, the full implications of his arrival beginning to hit her.

He sobered suddenly, all the amused mockery dying from his smooth, dark face. 'I had to see you because of Jessie.'

This was what Eden had feared. She had to think quickly. Something told her she was going to need all her wits about her! 'She—she's away.'

Diego kicked a pebble with unnecessary force and it hit the water with a plop. 'I heard she was. Where?'

'I'm afraid I can't tell you.'

'Can't or won't?'

When she stared at him with genuine uncertainty, he stared sullenly back. 'I heard about your marriage too. Done quite well for yourself, haven't you, young Eden? You grabbed at a good thing, yet you begrudge me the same chance.'

Eden's cheeks flamed as she met his frustrated gaze. Jessie might be better off without him. 'I don't have to listen to your insults!' She picked up her towel, throwing it around her shoulders like a cloak as she turned away from him.

Again he stepped neatly in front of her, stopping her. 'Eden, I'm sorry—I didn't mean to say that. I want your help, not your hate. I've been hanging around for days trying to see Jessie—my nerves aren't so good. I decided to find you, when I couldn't find Jessie, but when I heard indirectly that you were married, I daren't go near the plantation. I've been here five successive afternoons hoping to catch you if you came to see your father.'

'Don't you think you've left it a bit late?' she asked stonily.

'I still love her,' he said stubbornly.

Eden shook her head in bewilderment. 'You have a funny way of showing it! You deserted her, left her to fend for herself after crashing her car. I can't believe that's true devotion?'

'How did you know about that?' he asked, frowning.

'Jessie told me.' Eden wondered now if he was aware of what had happened after he left the car.

She was just about to enquire when he exclaimed, 'That wasn't my fault, though why she should tell you, after being so terrified of anyone knowing about it, beats me! We were running away together, did she tell you that? Vern had sacked me, so we knew we'd get no sympathy from him. Jessie went nearly crazy, she said it was the only way, and I couldn't go fast enough. She kept urging me on, then when the car crashed and her legs were caught she wouldn't let me stay. She said Vern would kill me, whether or not she was hurt. And if she was hurt she'd need his help. He would have to look after her.'

'Couldn't you have . . .?'

'Don't look at me like that, sweetheart,' he shrugged, 'I'm not the stuff heroes are made of. I panicked! For one thing, I had no money, to speak of—for another, I have a healthy respect for your husband's temper, when he's aroused.'

'Then why come back now?'

'I've come back,' he replied bleakly, 'because I still want her.'

CHAPTER TEN

EDEN looked past Diego, her eyes wandering blindly over the sands. In the distance a few crabs were scuttling about. There were seabirds swooping, finding scraps, enjoying themselves. Above their heads the sun beat down, yet Eden shivered. As Diego waited, a black scowl on his face, she hesitated. Did Jessie still want him? That seemed to Eden the important question, and how could anyone answer it but Jessie herself? And had anyone but Jessie the right to tell Diego to go and get lost? While Eden knew she had never cared for Diego Dexter, she had sometimes thought that Vern had come down unduly hard on his love affair with Jessie. After all, Jessie had been nearly thirty, surely old enough to know her own mind, and Diego wasn't without his good points. But if Jessie loved Martin Darel now, she mightn't want to see Diego again. Because of the past. Eden didn't think Jessie would want to see him anyway, and the shock might be bad for her.

'I can't promise to speak to Jessie about you,' she said at last.

'Then I'll have to see her myself.'

'No!' Eden couldn't take the responsibility for that! If he approached Jessie without warning, there was no knowing how she might react. 'Diego,' she asked shakily, 'could you be patient until she comes back? I don't know what I can say to her, but I promise I'll try and find out if she still cares for you.'

Diego watched her suspiciously as he considered this. 'You'd have to meet me afterwards and let me know, but I'm not sure I can trust you.'

Did everyone have to doubt her integrity? Eden

gazed at him bitterly. 'That's a risk you'll have to take, I'm afraid, but I have to warn you, Jessie's been very ill. She was badly injured in that car crash you ran from—she's still not a hundred per cent. If you aren't satisfied with the answer I bring, I can't stop you from approaching her yourself, so why should I lie to you?'

'You promise to pave the way?'

'I'm not saying that, but I do think she should have some warning.'

Diego, probably because Jessie was away and he had no idea where to find her, reluctantly agreed. 'I'll meet you a week today,' he said. 'That should give you ample time to find her and talk to her. I'll be on the road outside the plantation, and you'd better be there with some news for me!'

Eden was conscious of Joe throwing her anxious looks when she returned to have tea with him, but she had a lot on her mind. Diego's reappearance had both shocked and frightened her. She felt desperately in need of someone to turn to, while she knew there might be nothing anyone could do. She would be foolish, and selfish, to worry Joe with a problem he could do nothing about.

She hadn't told Diego that she'd got the blame for Jessie's accident. If she had, it might have put a weapon in his hands that he might have used. He might stop at nothing, including blackmail, if he was frustrated, and, Eden believed, if Jessie had to endure this and Vern found out, it would make him even more contemptuous than he already was of the girl he had married.

When Vern went out to dinner that evening, Eden was almost glad. He had said he was going out, but she had thought he might merely have been threatening to do so in order to hurt her, and when she heard him going she breathed a guilty sigh of relief. If she had had to sit opposite him at the dinner table he might have sensed something out of the ordinary was wrong and

wormed it out of her. By the morning she hoped to
have regained her composure and that her defences
would be stronger. Whatever happened he must never
suspect she had seen Diego.

She dined alone with Faith and listened while Vern's
aunt told her about his childhood.

'He was always a leader,' Faith smiled, 'always knew
exactly what he wanted since before he could walk. His
father didn't always manage his affairs very wisely. If
Vern hadn't been here things would have been much
worse than they are. You have a good husband, my
child. A lot of women would have liked to marry him,
but I always knew he would wait until he found a girl
he could love. The last two years in the States haven't
been easy for him. I don't know what it was eating
away at him, but I'm sure he's very happy now.'

Eden hoped Faith would never find out that Vern
was far from happy. She was brooding over this when
Faith surprised her by saying she would soon be
returning to the States. 'Oh, why?' she exclaimed,
knowing she would miss her.

'I really have to check my affairs,' Faith replied
ruefully, but with a warmth in her eyes which betrayed
that she was aware of Eden's dismay and appreciative.
'I'm not sure now that it's much good waiting for
Jessie. I think,' she leaned forward confidentially, 'she's
in love with Martin Darel, and it might be the best
thing that could happen if they were to marry. She likes
the States, though, so if I remove myself, she may be
able to decide on her future with a clearer mind.'

Eden pretended to be asleep when Vern came home.
It was almost dawn. She knew it was a long drive from
Kingston, if that was where he had been, but even so,
he couldn't have left until late. Eden had her eyes
closed, but she kept seeing him with Carita. He didn't
pause by her bed. If he had he might have seen the slow
tears forcing their way through Eden's tightly closed

lids, but he went straight to his dressing-room and closed the door.

At breakfast, unaware of the dark circles under her eyes, the unhappy droop to her mouth, she tried to talk to him calmly. She told him how Faith was thinking of going home—and her reasons. 'She believes it might be better if she just slipped away, but I'm sure Jessie won't think so.'

'I'll give Jessie a ring,' he agreed half impatiently. 'I wish I'd known this yesterday, I could have brought her back with me.'

'How was she?' Eden asked carefully.

'Very well,' he replied, without much apparent interest, his glance narrowed on Eden's pale face. 'How was Joe yesterday?'

'How did you know I'd been to see him?'

'Mrs Prince told me.'

'He was fine,' she said, then was horrified to find herself flushing vividly as she suddenly thought of Diego.

When Vern stared at her suspiciously she wasn't surprised. 'You look guilty. Why?'

'I'm not,' she retorted quite truthfully, unless she was guilty of keeping her meeting with Diego from him.

For a moment Vern paused, as if fighting with intuition. 'I told you not to walk.'

'I needed the exercise.'

'Don't do it again.'

Eden stared mutely at the tablecloth as he rose to his feet, wondering if it were possible to feel more miserable. He towered over her, so tall and broad she felt dwarfed, yet she couldn't be unaware of the sheer masculine appeal which set her heart racing.

'I'll see you later,' he said coolly, as though she was a stranger.

He rang Jessie and, for once, Eden knew she must have judged correctly when Jessie hurried home in person to say goodbye to her aunt. When Martin came with her and announced their engagement, Faith left happily, quite overcome by joy.

Martin could only stay one night because of pressure of business and Jessie didn't return to Kingston with him. She decided at the last minute to stay at home and begin drawing up guest lists for her wedding. Eden spent an agonising day wondering how she was going to tell her about Diego, or whether to tell her at all.

Jessie appeared to be avoiding her, but the next afternoon, having decided she must say something, Eden found her alone in the drawing-room. She was due to meet Diego the following day and guessed that if she wasn't there Diego would arrive at the plantation. And, if this happened, Jessie might never forgive her for not warning her. She had been tempted not to say anything—just to go and tell Diego simply that Jessie was engaged to another man and appeal to him to go away without causing any more trouble, but how could she be sure of Diego being prepared to accept that? He might only sweep her aside and rush here to confront Jessie himself.

'What is it?' Jessie snapped impatiently, raising her head from the notes she was making.

Realising she was unwelcome, Eden paused uncertainly, her eyes anxious. 'I'd like a word with you, Jessie.'

'Come in, then!' Jessie snapped ungraciously. 'I wish you'd stop creeping around like a ghost. Can you wonder that Vern's tired of you already?'

'How can you say such a thing?' Eden whispered miserably.

'I have eyes, haven't I?' the other girl retorted sharply. 'You're far too young for him, for one thing. Carita thinks it's a pity he realised this too late. Of course she knows he's considering a divorce, but that takes time.'

Eden went cold as she feared Jessie could be right. All the signs were there that Vern wanted to get rid of her, and he must have been discussing divorce with Carita. 'I'd rather not talk about it,' she said tautly.

Jessie shrugged indifferently, yet her eyes kept returning to Eden's white face and her own seemed to lose a little colour. 'Eden . . .?' she began tentatively.

Eden didn't hear the reluctant remorse in Jessie's voice. She just wanted to say what she had to say and escape. 'While you were at Kingston,' she interrupted unintentionally, 'I saw Diego Dexter.'

'Who?' Jessie gasped, her lips suddenly bloodless.

'Diego—you heard,' Eden retorted unevenly. 'He was asking about you. He says he still loves you.'

'Where is he?' Jessie, clearly shocked, glanced around wildly, as if expecting him to appear any moment.

All her cool confidence appeared to have left her, but Eden could feel little sympathy. 'I don't know where he is now, but he waylaid me on the beach, one day, when I was visiting Dad.'

'Did your father see him?'

'No.'

'Well, I have no wish to see him again!' Jessie's voice rose shrilly. 'He was in love with you, not me, and if he tries to make anyone believe otherwise, I'll deny everything. I don't want to hear Diego Dexter's name mentioned again. Once you're rid of Vern you can go off with him! I don't care what you do!'

Jessie, collapsing hysterically, was sobbing wildly when Vern strode in. Immediately he tried to console his sister. 'You'd better go to your room, Eden,' he ordered.

Eden gazed at him numbly. As always, he was blaming her because Jessie was upset. His face was grey, his green eyes utterly condemning, and she wondered unhappily what was to happen next. It couldn't be much fun, having two women fighting round him. He must be looking forward to the time when he was rid of them both and Carita was here, as his wife.

'I'm sorry,' she mumbled, when he came to find her later, and she braced herself to suffer his disapproval.

He threw off his sweat-soaked shirt on his way to his room. 'I won't put up with much more of it, I'm warning you!'

'I've said I'm sorry, haven't I?' Swinging round, with more defiance than she normally showed, she halted at the pulse-stopping vista of his bare, hair-covered chest. 'Vern,' she whispered, closing her eyes as the room suddenly spun.

As she swayed he shot a hand out to steady her. He was far from gentle, however, and his voice held no hint of sympathy as he rasped, 'If you will agitate yourself and others. what more can you expect?'

'It wasn't that . . .' How could she explain the wanton urge she had felt to be in his arms again? Yet she loved him so much it wasn't only physical, although its effect made her tremble.

He didn't let her go immediately. He hesitated, his eyes glittering on her bent head. She could feel his glance almost tearing her apart, as if he was looking for something. 'Eden,' he said roughly, 'do you want a divorce?'

Jessie had said it was Vern who wanted one. Was he waiting for her to take the initiative so he wouldn't feel guilty? Eden's cheeks flushed unhappily as she tilted her chin to gaze up at him. 'Do you?'

He sighed at her evasion but didn't answer directly himself. 'Sometimes I think it might be the best thing.'

Eden wanted to refute this wildly. She wanted to cling to him tightly, so he could never escape, but she knew that would never be sufficient to hold a man like him. She'd had her chance and failed and would soon have to let him go—she realised that.

Suddenly, without warning, he pulled her to him and

began kissing her savagely. She was unprepared for it and because of the anger she could still feel in him she tried to fight him. But as his mouth crushed hers hotly, her hunger for him burst through the control she tried to place on it, and her slender body shuddered as her response quickened. Soon she was responding with a passion she couldn't restrain, the sheer intensity of their mutual desire sending flames over her skin. When he as suddenly thrust her from him with a muttered curse and slammed out of the room, she cried as if her heart would break. This must be his way of punishing her before he left her for Carita.

It was easier than she had thought it might be to get away to meet Diego. Vern had gone to Montego Bay and had told Mrs Prince he didn't expect to be home before early evening. As he had scarcely spoken to her since the previous afternoon, she didn't think he would be interested in what she was doing anyway.

After lunch she slipped out, and Diego was waiting where he had promised he would be. He had pulled off the road to park on the verge and was standing beside his car. As she drew nearer, she reflected, with his dark Spanish looks, he was a lot more handsome than Martin Darel, but Jessie must have realised in time that Martin was the better man.

'Should you be standing out here?' she asked, breathless from hurrying as she paused beside him. 'Anyone might see you!'

'I'm not a criminal,' he retorted, staying exactly where he was, his eyes intent on her hot face. 'Well?'

Realising his belligerence covered a rather pathetic eagerness didn't make answering any easier. If he really loved Jessie as much as he thought he did, she felt sorry for him.

'Couldn't we sit inside first?' she begged hastily, as he looked ready to shake an answer out of her.

'If you like,' he submitted impatiently, but once in

the car he soon made it clear he was prepared to make no more concessions. 'Come on now,' he glared, 'let's have it! I suspect from your face that the news isn't good, but I'm not waiting any longer.'

Eden, despite the roughness of his voice, was suddenly swamped with pity. 'Jessie came home engaged to another man,' she told him gently. 'She's sorry, but she doesn't want to see you again. I think she feels there wouldn't be much point,' she improvised quickly.

Diego was silent for a few bitter moments, then asked tersely, 'Who is this other man?'

Evasion seemed senseless. 'Martin Darel. He's in business in Kingston. Do you know him?'

Diego shook his head. 'And she loves him?'

'She must do.'

'I don't believe it.'

Eden glanced at him nervously. 'I'm sorry, but whether you believe it or not, Mr Dexter, there's nothing you can do about it.'

'Isn't there?'

'No.' She tried not to be alarmed by the harsh anger in his voice. 'I think if I were you I'd just forget all about her.'

'But you aren't me!' he snarled. 'Therein lies the difference!'

As Eden glanced away from him, hating to witness his distress, her eyes widened in dismay as she caught sight of Vern passing them. He looked straight at them, though in a blank way that told her they might have a breathing space, however brief, before he suddenly realised who they were.

Her hand flew, reflecting her fright, to the car door. 'I must go, Diego. That was . . .'

'No need to tell me who it was!' Almost pushing her from the car, he switched the ignition. 'There's nothing wrong with my eyesight, at least, and I have no wish to meet Mr Lomax!'

Not apparently noticing how his rough thrust made Eden nearly fall, he roared away, leaving her to face her furious husband alone. Vern had turned on a hair's-breadth, to screech up behind him.

He could have caught Diego, Eden knew, but he chose to pounce on her instead. In a flash he was beside her, grasping her fiercely, his breathing uneven, as though he had been running.

'So this is what you get up to, each time you're supposed to be seeing Joe?'

He was livid. His face had a hard, suppressed look, as if the anger was locked into his cheekbones. Beneath his skin was a flush of dark red. Eden stared at him, the fear overwhelming her mirrored in her widening eyes. What was he going to do?

She didn't have long to wait to find out. As she watched in stunned silence, he thrust her ruthlessly into his car and got in beside her. At least he was sparing her the indignity of a good shaking on the highway, she thought hollowly, while wondering if it wasn't something more like murder he had on his mind.

'How long have you been meeting Dexter?' he rapped, his eyes black with fury.

'I—I've only seen him twice,' she stammered, 'but I didn't seek him out.'

'Don't give me that!' he said savagely. 'I knew you were up to something, but I thought you'd stopped hankering after other men. I can only imagine you're insatiable!'

She flushed to the roots of her hair. Did he have to be so cruel? 'Vern,' she was suddenly very desperate, 'Diego means nothing to me. You have to believe it!'

'Then why were you here today?' he rasped, his face contemptuous. 'Don't try to tell me you met him sheerly by accident?'

'No . . .' She gazed at him, her eyes full of painful frustration; she couldn't tell him that. A sob caught her throat as she suddenly realised what a mess she was in. She couldn't explain about Jessie and Diego without confessing everything, and, even if that had been possible, Vern wouldn't believe her.

'The—the other day,' she faltered, 'he asked me to try and help him. I had to see him again to tell him I can't . . .'

Vern turned on her, his eyes blazing. 'You'd better shut up, Eden. I've been a fool, but I certainly don't need to go on being one. Once I thought our marriage had a chance of succeeding, but I find I'm mistaken. You'd better go back to your father and I'll get in touch with my solicitor.'

Eden might have been delivered a physical blow. She felt faint, all the blood seeming to leave her body. Yet she could only murmur stupidly, 'Your solicitor?'

'Don't look so bewildered,' his mouth twisted, 'I'll give you a divorce. You can feel free from now on to continue your interesting relationship with Dexter.'

'No, Vern!' Hysterically she grabbed his arm, but he shook her off, disregarding her anguished expression.

'You won't have a thing to worry about, Eden. The land deal's gone through. The agreement's signed and tied up, so our divorce won't affect your father. After he's gone, his income will continue for you, only I don't promise to let you remain in the house.'

Eden failed to take it in. She couldn't believe Vern really meant to get rid of her. Jessie had warned her, she should have been prepared but she wasn't. It was a great shock. She heard his voice commanding her grimly to stay away from the plantation—warning her against making any more trouble. Her ears began to ring, so she couldn't seem to hear the half of what he was saying.

Tears were rolling down her cheeks before he appeared to notice she wasn't following him. Coldly he snapped, 'It's no use talking any more. Anything further we have to say to each other can be said through my solicitor.'

'Vern,' she whispered huskily, 'I love you.'

'For heaven's sake, Eden!' his hands clenched, as if he would liked to have hit her, 'you know as well as I do it doesn't mean a thing!'

Eden shivered, a terrible chill encompassing her as she realised she had gambled and lost. He had never pretended to love her, as she constantly reminded herself.

'When do you want me to go?' she asked unsteadily.

He wrenched his eyes from her tear-stained face. 'I'll take you back to your father now and send someone along with your things later.'

'That won't be necessary, Vern.' She tried to speak with a little pride, though her voice still trembled. 'You paid for most of my new clothes. You can keep them.'

'Don't be so damned stupid!' he retorted, turning the car violently. 'Do you think I need a constant reminder of a wife I'd rather forget?'

Eden felt ill for several days until she eventually, if painfully, adjusted. If it hadn't been for Joe, she often wondered if she would ever have survived. It was out of gratitude, and for his sake, that she tried to put the past behind her, but it wasn't easy to pretend she was beginning to look forward instead of back. She suspected she didn't altogether fool Joe, although he stopped fussing so much when she didn't eat and he didn't ask quite so frequently how she was feeling.

She told him that her marriage hadn't worked out, that Vern had found someone else. To begin with, Joe had been furious, until she had managed to convince him that Vern had married her chiefly because of the land and Jessie.

'The land was important to him and he thought it would help if you knew I was safe. He also wanted someone he could rely on as company for Jessie. No one could foresee that they would both fall in love, Dad.'

Joe hadn't argued, although he had wanted to go and confront Vern himself, but Eden wouldn't let him. She prayed that he would eventually accept what she hadn't been able to tell him and stop looking at her with a kind of frustrated anxiety in his eyes.

She tried to pick up the threads of her old life where she had left off before she was married, but her enthusiasm for the things she used to do had disappeared. Even the reefs seemed to have lost their old enchantment, although she spent hours sitting on the sands, staring out to sea. Diego Dexter didn't try and see her again, and she sometimes wondered if he had ever tried to get in touch with Jessie. Of Vern she heard nothing, not even through his solicitor.

Then, one evening, the torment within her changed to a pain of a different kind. She had spent the day decorating the living-room, giving it a fresh coat of paint, and Joe blamed this. He had given her aspirin and a hot drink, but in the middle of the night, when the pain in Eden's stomach flared excruciatingly, he had grown alarmed and taken her to hospital. As they had no car he had had to ring for a taxi, and it hadn't been easy to get one at that hour. By the time they had arrived at the hospital it had almost been too late.

The operation was a success, but there were complications and Eden was seriously ill. When she recovered sufficiently to be conscious of what was going on about her, they told her her husband was waiting to see her, but she became quite hysterical and refused to see him. She wanted her father and no one else.

Joe was so overcome he couldn't speak. He held her hand and kept patting it while he gazed at her anxiously. Eventually he said, 'I had to tell Vern—he's still your husband, you know. He's been worried out of his head.'

'I don't want to see him.'

Joe swallowed, the sight of his daughter's white, shadowed face on the pillows moving him deeply. 'We've both been worried, darling. These past two days have been hell. We've prayed for you.'

Dry-eyed, Eden looked at him, her cheeks burning. 'I'm sorry, Dad.'

'Here,' Joe swallowed again, 'the doc said only five minutes, so I'd better give you this. They've advised Vern to come back tomorrow. I thought he was going to barge in here regardless, but instead he wrote you this.'

She stared at it without interest, feeling strangely remote. 'I can't see it properly, Dad.'

Joe blinked and tried to get rid of the lump in his throat. 'I could hold it up for you.'

'If you like.' It was more to please Joe that she agreed, yet inside her something fluttered, the first faint spark of life she had felt for days.

Joe held the note in front of her but didn't look at it. She read—'Eden, I love you. I want you to know this and hope it will make you want to read on. When Joe told me how ill you were I realised you are the only thing that matters—life without you isn't worth living. I don't care what you've done. I only know I no longer believe you are capable of doing anything wrong. I'm the one in the wrong for ever doubting you. I hope you can forgive me enough to let me see you, to ask your forgiveness personally. Vern.'

Eden lay very still then looked up at Joe, her eyes swimming. 'Oh, Dad . . .'

Joe was just about to call the doctor when he saw she was smiling tremulously through her tears. 'Tell Vern I'll see him in a few days,' she whispered, and with his note clutched tightly in her hands she fell asleep.

The nurses told Joe it was the first real sleep she had had, and from that moment she began to recover. She refused to see Vern though until she was home again and she was grateful he didn't insist, although he rang several times a day to ask how she was. She had her reasons for not seeing him, she told a puzzled Joe, but wouldn't reveal what they were. It wasn't until she left hospital and Vern still stayed away that she began to worry.

Having come home almost fully recovered, when she began looking pale again, Joe grew increasingly concerned. 'Why don't you give Vern a ring?' he suggested. 'You never actually answered his note, although I gave him your message. Perhaps he's waiting for you to speak to him yourself.'

'He could have changed his mind,' she said heavily, 'He might have discovered he doesn't love me after all.'

'Isn't it worth trying to find out?'

'I don't know, Dad,' she sighed. 'When someone is rushed to hospital, as I was, people often say and do things they don't always mean. That's why I wouldn't see him—I wanted him to be sure. I shouldn't like him to feel he was committed by something he only said on impulse, because he was sorry for me.'

It was a week before Vern came, and by this time Eden had given up expecting him and was back in the dull, apathetic state she had been in before. On this particular evening she had wandered along the beach and was sitting in her favourite spot, gazing out to sea, when he found her. When she heard him coming she turned her head, her eyes widening apprehensively.

They stared at each other silently. Vern had changed, he had lost weight, his face was gaunt and drawn, his eyes full with pain. His pain seemed to communicate with her own as he dropped suddenly beside her.

'Oh, Vern!' she choked, burying her face in her hands. 'Where have you been?'

Gently he prized her fingers from tear-wet cheeks, then she was in his arms and he was holding her as tightly as he dared, for fear of hurting her. 'Darling,' he groaned, 'if only you knew the willpower it took to stay away!'

'Why did you wait so long?' she whispered against his broad chest. She could feel his heart thundering under her cheek, his whole body trembling.

'I nearly didn't come at all,' he muttered harshly, 'not after what Jessie, then Dexter, confessed to.'

Eden went very still, then she raised her face to look at him, the bright colour which had fleetingly touched her skin receding.

'It was nothing I shouldn't have guessed for myself,' he went on bitterly, before she could find the right words to ask what he meant. 'When I think of the pain we've caused you needlessly, I can feel nothing but contempt—for the three of us!'

His vehemence frightened her. 'What did they tell you?' she whispered.

'Everything.'

'Everything?' she echoed in startled bewilderment, as his arms tightened.

'Yes,' he nodded grimly, leaning back against a boulder, so he could hold her more closely. 'Jessie began behaving oddly after you went. She wouldn't go ahead with her wedding plans, although I told her to. The night Joe phoned and said you'd had an operation for appendicitis and there were complications, I didn't wake her. I rushed straight to the hospital, but when I got home again, after you'd refused to see me, and I must have looked as terrible as I felt, she broke down completely and told me all she'd done.'

Curiously, Eden felt nothing but surprise. 'Why should she do that?' she wondered aloud.

Vern shrugged bleakly. 'What she didn't tell me, I got out of her. She went right back to her former visit here, when you were eighteen. Just before I arrived and dragged you out of the sea, remember?'

As Eden flushed slightly and murmured yes, he

continued, 'I was busy in the States and she wouldn't wait until I could come with her. Since our parents died I've always tried to keep an eye on her, but she was twenty-eight, scarcely a child, and when she insisted, I gave in. I realise now that Dexter was the attraction. I didn't then.'

'Why didn't you like him?' Eden asked slowly, as he paused.

'I wasn't satisfied with his overall performance,' Vern replied curtly. 'I'd left him in charge of the plantation and there were several things that didn't add up. Jessie knew this, but I don't remember feeling any personal animosity towards him, not until I saw him looking at you.'

'He wasn't interested in me.'

'I know that now,' Vern said savagely, 'although I don't believe he was entirely indifferent.'

Eden drew a deep breath, shaken by the sudden rage on his face. 'What exactly did Jessie say?' she asked hurriedly. 'You don't need to go into details.'

'No,' his mouth twisted, 'you must be very familiar with those. She told me how she'd thought my dislike of Dexter was greater than it actually was and that she'd deliberately cultivated your friendship and asked you to the plantation in order to make me believe, if there was any trouble, that it was you whom Dexter was interested in. By throwing the two of you together occasionally, she hoped to give this impression and hoodwink me. And,' he added grimly, 'you'll recall that I was furious when you mentioned about losing your dinghy and how she had rescued you from the caves? Well, apparently it was she who cut your boat loose in the first place. She'd seen you going there and thought it would be a chance of getting you in her debt.'

Eden was stunned. 'I didn't know about that.'

'That's not all,' he assured her bitterly. 'When she discovered I was taking you out, it seems she didn't like it. She admits to being jealous, though don't ask me why, because we've never been very close. I believe she came here and talked a lot of nonsense about Carita Darel and a girl in the States. I had affairs with plenty of women, Eden, before I met you, but neither Carita nor Rona Trent, who lives in New York, were among them. I've never been in love before and certainly never asked anyone to marry me. I only wish I'd been here that morning she came to see you!'

Eden ran a loving hand along his cheek, her pulses leaping as he muttered that he adored her against her hair and she realised he was almost forcibly stopping himself from kissing her.

'I was roaming the hills later that day,' she whispered unevenly. 'I felt so miserable and confused after what Jessie told me, I scarcely knew what I was doing. I was watching the road, hoping to avoid you if you called here on your way from Kingston, and I saw both you and Diego at the same time. He had Jessie with him and I thought I owed it to her to warn her. She'd told me, you see, that you didn't approve of him.'

'And she pushed you in his car.'

Eden nodded reluctantly.

Vern's voice came even harsher. 'When she told me the truth about that and her accident, I could have killed her! Apparently she hadn't realised she didn't love Dexter until she was running away with him and used the crash as a kind of heaven-sent opportunity to get rid of him. When you came along it seemed that fate was playing right into her hands and she grasped the chance of involving you. That way, she not only managed to get rid of you, too, but it gave the impression that she was the innocent party. I could kill my own sister,' he groaned. 'but why didn't you tell me the truth?'

'Would you have believed me?' Eden's voice trembled. 'I was caught in a trap.'

'Can you ever forgive me?' Vern muttered tensely.

'Easily,' Eden assured him, her eyes gentle with love.

'I don't deserve you,' he breathed, holding her tightly, his mouth opening over hers, the restraint he was obviously exercising slipping badly as he kissed her passionately.

'I found Dexter,' he said much later, but with a determination which made Eden aware there were still a few things he felt he had to say. 'He admitted everything of importance and a lot more besides.'

'I think he still loves Jessie,' Eden sighed. 'He asked me to speak to her on his behalf. He threatened to come to the plantation, and I didn't know what to do, but when she came home engaged to Martin, she refused to see him. When you found me with him, I was advising him to go away and forget her.'

'I'm afraid I'm not interested in what either he or Jessie does any more,' Vern spoke with a curtness that was distinctly chilling. 'Jessie has gone to the States to stay with Faith. She'll be married from there, but I've told her we won't be at the wedding.'

'Oh, but,' Eden glanced at him uncertainly, 'if she's sorry . . .?'

'Eden!' Vern's eyes hardened in angry amazement. 'Don't tell me you can forgive her, after all she's done!'

'I think eventually we might forget,' Eden said softly. 'Life's too short to bear grudges.'

Vern's voice thickened. 'I'm not promising anything. I still don't understand how you can even forgive me.'

'I love you,' Eden replied simply, 'and it wasn't altogether your fault that you misjudged me. All the evidence was against me, but you did say, in the note you wrote me in hospital, before Jessie told you the truth, that you believed in me.'

'It wasn't so much what I thought you'd done,' he groaned. 'When I caught you in the car, two years ago with Dexter, you weren't committing a criminal offence.

I loved you so much I was in a blind rage. I hadn't been able to stop thinking of you since the night of your eighteenth birthday, but I thought you were too young to know your own mind. Catching you with Dexter seemed to prove I was right and the part you appeared to have played in Jessie's accident only seemed to confirm it.'

'I loved you then.'

'Oh, my darling,' he groaned, claiming her lips once more then burying his face in her soft neck. 'I love you so much—and the time I've wasted over my infernal jealousy! I tried to stay in the States, but I had to return. I was as desperate for the sight of you as a man is for water in the desert. When I saw you dancing with other men at the Club dance, I knew I hadn't been imagining the strength of my feelings, but I was too proud to climb down. I wanted you, but I had to use Joe and the land as an excuse to get you. Our honeymoon was both a delight and torture, having to pretend my feelings weren't involved.'

'You were very cool,' she sighed, remembering.

'Because it was either that or going to the other extreme, and I didn't want to frighten you. If I'd known you loved me,' he tilted up her chin, his mouth briefly teasing while his eyes smouldered, 'things would have been very different! As it was, you tantalised me more than enough, you little witch!'

'How am I to believe you love me when you call me that?' Eden murmured in the same tone, while wondering incredulously if she wasn't dreaming.

'I'm going to spend the rest of my life convincing you,' Vern said huskily, his slight smile fading as he began kissing her again, this time with barely restrained passion.

Eden's heart leapt as one of his hands slid down her back, pressing her tightly against him, making her burningly conscious of his hard, flat muscles. Her lips parted passionately under the pressure of his and her arms fluttered helplessly to his broad shoulders, winding their way around his neck.

She made no effort to resist as he tugged her shirt from her jeans and began slowly caressing her sensitised skin. When he reached her breasts, she could feel her taut nipples pressing the palms of his hands and a sharp gasp escaped her. As his head dropped and his tongue explored sensuously, she trembled in every inch of her body.

The emotion clamping them together was devastating, an immeasurable thing, driving Vern hungrily on. When he paused to look at her, his eyes were concerned but dark with the depth of his desire. 'How well are you, my love?' he asked thickly.

'I'm not sure.' She stirred reluctantly as he waited for an answer. Then with soft eagerness, her eyes shyly met his. 'I'm not sure how I am, but I know how I feel.'

'Oh, darling!' His arms tightened and she thought for a moment he was going to forget she had been ill and bring their lovemaking to the natural conclusion for which they both yearned. The beach was deserted, they were completely alone and they were man and wife.

When, with obvious regret, Vern sighed and rose slowly to his feet, lifting her with him, she felt deprived and didn't bother to hide it.

He smiled soberly as he understood her fleeting resentment. 'I see I'm going to have to be strong for both of us,' he said, with a teasing wryness, still holding her, 'but if I'm to restrain myself for a few more days, my wanton wife, at least I intend having you with me. My bed's been so lonely, I've scarcely slept since you left me. Do you think Joe would forgive me if I took you straight home?'

Eden, struggling out of the sensuous cloud which had

enveloped her, snuggled against him with a contented sigh. 'I think it's what he wants most,' she said simply, feeling, as Vern turned to carry her back along the beach with easy strides, that at last all her dreams were coming true.

Harlequin® Plus

A WORD ABOUT THE AUTHOR

Margaret Pargeter was born in the quiet Northumbrian Valley, in the extreme northeast of England, where she lives today.

When did she first feel an urge to write? "Truthfully, I can't recall," she admits. "It must have been during my early teens. I remember carrying a notebook in my pocket, and while milking cows I would often take a break to scribble something down."

The jottings developed into short stories, and Margaret's first break came several years after she had married. Her husband talked her into entering a writing contest, and her work caught the eye of an editor, who asked her to write serial stories. From there she went on to complete her first romance novel, *Winds from the Sea* (Romance #1899).

Among the author's many blessings, which she likes to keep counting, is the "pleasure I get from knowing that people enjoy reading my books. And," she adds, "I hope they long continue to do so."